Harrow and Harvest

Books by Barbara Willard

Harrow and Harvest

Barbara Willard

E. P. Dutton & Co., Inc.   New York

First published in the U.S.A. 1975 by E. P. Dutton & Co., Inc.
Copyright © 1974 by Barbara Willard

LIBRARY OF CONGRESS CATALOGING IN PUBLICATION DATA

Willard, Barbara   Harrow and harvest

SUMMARY: The Medley family and their
ancestral home, Mantlemass, are drawn into the conflict
of the English Civil War.

1. Great Britain—History—Civil War, 1642–1649—
Juvenile fiction. [1. Great Britain—History—
Civil War, 1642–1649—Fiction]   I. Title.
PZ7.W6547Har3 [Fic]   75-11918   ISBN 0-525-31505-5

Printed in the U.S.A.   First Edition
10 9 8 7 6 5 4 3 2 1

Contents

I

The End of a World

'Go now,' the dying man said. 'Take Harry and go – now, now . . .'

Edmund held his father's hand and asked 'Where?' He watched the struggle in a face changing with every second. He knew he must be patient, that there could be no forcing an answer, for there was only strength left for just so much. He began to dread that the most important words might never be spoken.

The boy crouched down and put his own face close, lest he should miss some final sighing message. His father was lying where he had fallen, after he had staggered indoors and up the stairs when the trooper shot him shamefully in the back. There was a good deal of blood, but Edmund was somehow more concerned with the sweat that had poured down his father's face, and which now, checked, lay puddling along the neat line of his beard and in the hollows behind his nostrils. Edmund pulled off his neckcloth and mopped at the sweat in a helpless, hopeless manner.

Behind him he heard Harry suddenly start to cry, and he shushed him impatiently.

'Tell me where, father,' Edmund urged, but gently. 'Where must I take Harry, sir?'

'They'll burn down Ravenshall, Ned . . .'

'Aye – but where must we go then? Whatever you tell me, I swear to do it. But where – *where* would you have us go?'

There was a long, long silence – or it seemed long to Edmund. He almost accepted that it was too late now for his father to give any order or advice. Then suddenly the strange eyes flew open, and they were clear and almost smiling.

'Your mother . . .' he began. Then he said quite loudly, 'The ten-acre.' And then, on a fresh, shallow breath, 'The book I showed you – take that. The secret, Ned. Go to Mantlemass. Take the book back to Mantlemass . . .'

After that he was indeed lost to them for ever.

Edmund's hand was quite steady as he laid it over his father's eyes and closed the lids. He kissed him on the brow and cheeks and set his hands to look restful on his breast. A man of less than forty, handsome, strong, it was hard to believe he could never rise and walk away from this room.

'Say good-bye,' Edmund ordered his young brother. He wondered briefly if he should take the big seal ring from his father's hand – but he could not bring himself to do it. 'Save snivelling for later. Kiss him and be done. I have to think. I have to think very hard.' He looked sideways at Harry and the grief and terror in the boy's face almost defeated him. Edmund was not yet fifteen, his brother was just twelve, and there was man's work to be done. 'We'll not save ourselves by bawling,' he said harshly.

'What can come to us?' sobbed Harry. 'We've no living kin.'

'We have each other.'

' "Your mother," he said.'

'God rest both. They'll be together for sure, Harry.'

Harry caught at Edmund's arm and clung to it, and tried to check his tears. The effort set him shivering, his teeth chattered.

'Let me think now,' Edmund urged, shaking him to rally him, if that were possible. 'There are cousins of some kind – at Mantlemass. You know that. You remember that, Harry – don't you?'

'Never seen! And that place is half of England away.'

'Well, then, there'll be much to see on the journey.'

'Shan't we better stay here and be killed like the rest? Like our poor father and the servants?'

'No, we shall not! Well – you stay, if you choose,' said Edmund carelessly. 'I'll be on my way.'

8

He turned away sharply, for his brother had fished up from somewhere a quick, sheepish grin, and it was sadder on his young face than tears.

'Listen,' the older brother said, speaking low and fast. 'We have to leave him lying here. There's no way for us to bury him. You understand, don't you?'

Harry nodded. 'He'll not be alone.'

'No, indeed,' said Edmund bitterly. 'Indeed not. There's half a dozen to keep him company.'

'Who, Ned? I dursen't go looking to see.'

'Hubert and Tom. Poor old Will. Martin that was too deaf to hear 'em coming. Even Margery and Nan, brother. They say women're safe with Parliament troopers – but this time it was different . . .' His voice trailed away and he struggled not to join in his brother's tears. Margery had been their nurse; Nan had sat all night through for nights on end with their mother when she was dying.

'The others ran away,' Harry said. He mumbled it, for to admit this was almost worst of all. They had seemed such loyal servants, so devoted and ready. 'Even Barnaby, Ned?'

Edmund did not answer that, he could not bear to. Of all men in the world, Barnaby had seemed the most rock-like. Edmund changed the subject by repeating something that his father had said – that the house would be burnt down for sure.

Outside, somewhere below, there was already much shouting. The boys were in the library, above the hall. As their father ran in, he had herded them before him and somehow dragged himself up the flight of stairs, slamming and bolting the library door before he fell. By some blessing, none had followed, the raiders being entirely concerned with their purpose of rounding up all available horses and their equipment. Edmund peered down cautiously from the high library window. Half a dozen troopers had been left behind, and now they were lugging out straw from the stables, to set against the doors of the house, and one had rolled out a barrel of tar to help the business on.

'We'll get out by the gateway stair, Harry.'

He realized how sharply and cleverly their father had thought in those few moments of disaster. This was the one room in the house they could escape by and none the wiser. It must have been

9

a plan already laid, for the times being what they were, a man of sense did think ahead how to act for the best in any sudden moment of crisis. It was hard to believe that the troopers had clattered in not much more than an hour ago, for all eternity seemed to stretch between that moment and this. Their own nearest neighbour, Mr Wormald, had been at the head of the troop, and his men had called him *Colonel*. Everyone had known he was for the Parliament, but he had always been an easy pleasant man. No one could have anticipated that he should come in his new guise and commandeer every horse he could find. Men change with the demands of their times. He had the animals rounded up and the stables emptied almost before the Ravenshall people knew what was happening. Then he had clattered off as if he could not quite bring himself to face any one of them. At the moment that the boy's father came from the house, his favourite riding horse, Apollo, was being led away. That was when the scuffle broke out, turning to a pitched battle with the weapons all on one side. And that was when the servants – some, like the two women, accidentally caught up in the fray – either fell or took to their heels. Stooping over old Will, who had served him and his father for sixty years, the master of the house took a shot in the back . . .

'They'll burn the place to hide what they've done,' Edmund muttered. 'Any other room in the house but here and we'd be trapped.'

'We'll not get far on foot, Ned – how could we?'

Edmund just managed to smile. 'What did our·father say – all but last of all? The ten-acre, he said. And there's Dryad and Lass and Psyche at grass there – far out of sight of the house – quite hidden . . . Now don't go yapping any more, Harry. I tell you, I have to think.'

'We can't stay till they set the house afire!'

'There's something I have to find.'

'Hurry, then, Ned! Hurry! Is it money?'

'That, too. Most important – the book.'

'Book! Are we to be burnt alive for a book?'

'You heard what he said. Take it to Mantlemass. Take the book back to Mantlemass, he said. Now – keep at the window. Watch how things go. I'll find it soon enough.'

He spoke with far more confidence than he could feel. It was already some time since his father had shown him the book – lost to their part of the family for many years, he had said, and then regained. It was very old indeed, perhaps two hundred years old. It held a secret that should be told to Edmund when he was grown a few more years. What the boy remembered most clearly was one of several papers folded between the pages. On it was roughly drawn the outline of a house, and on the reverse was a map, the place of the house marked. The house was Mantlemass, that he must now seek out as his father had ordered him. But how he was to find it unless he had the map, Edmund had no notion.

He began running his finger along the shelves, very well stocked for the house of a modest country gentleman. He could not remember what the book looked like, save that it was small, and his anxiety made it difficult to concentrate on the rows of leather spines.

'More straw,' Harry reported.

Edmund felt deeply frightened for the first time. Until now he had been calm because he must, and because it had barely struck home to him that he was now the head of a family of two, and all plans and decisions must be his to make. In its first stages the disaster had been full of such awful drama that it had kept him in a state of high nervous excitement that supported and strengthened him.

'Ned!'

'What now?'

'I think they'll light it soon.'

'Houses don't burn flat in a few minutes.'

'Oh hurry, hurry, do! What if we leave it too late? What then?'

Edmund knew what then. His brother's wavering voice almost made him decide to give up searching. He went to the window and stood by Harry, peering down, but standing carefully, afraid of being seen. What he saw filled him with terror. The straw piled against the walls, the tar now poured from its barrel over timbers dragged from the stables were not enough, it seemed. He was fairly sure they were preparing to use gunpowder, for they were laying some sort of a trail across the yard.

'Get on your way, Harry. I'll have one more look and join you.'

'I'll not go alone!'

'You'll do what you're bid. Go straight on to the passageway. I'll be with you before you count to a hundred.'

'I'll count it here,' Harry said.

Edmund was sick with indecision. Was this a moment that demanded immediate, naked flight – or would their state be even worse if he went without the directions that he sought? Better to live than die – and as he looked down into the yard he saw that they were just carting up the little keg of powder that held power enough to send Ravenshall to destruction.

Suddenly that small tight barrel, with its iron bindings, gave him what he needed. It reminded him sharply of the iron-bound chest that stood against the wall of the library closet. In that he would at least find money. Should he stay to get the key or run, now, for safety? The key, he knew, was small – small enough to be kept in a leather pouch with a velvet lining that hung on a belt at his father's waist. Remembering this, Edmund shivered.

'What's happening now, Harry?'

'I think they've all gone away,' Harry said, in a puzzled voice.

'Aye – they would do.'

'Would they?'

'They'll want to blow the house up, not themselves.'

'Let's go – let's go!'

Shuddering and apologetic, Edmund was groping for the key, trying not to look his dead father in the face. Then he had it, he was running to the closet and dragging out the box, fumbling the key into the lock and turning it with difficulty because his hands were trembling. He flung back the lid while Harry thumped him on the shoulders in frenzy, crying 'We must go! We must *go*!'

There were many things in the chest, but on top of all were two money bags and the book – small, shabby, a little leather-covered volume of Latin poems. He opened it and two papers fell out. One he shoved back, but the second was the map.

'We can leave now, Harry,' Edmund Medley said.

At the back of the closet where the chest was kept, a foot or two of panelling slid to disclose an opening. Beyond was a little cramped chamber – a priests' hole, it was called. There, the boy's father had told them, his grandmother who had been a firm Papist had concealed many Catholic priests on the run from a stern and cruel law. After her death it had not been used again, and it was damp and cobwebby and sad. Edmund and Harry had once or twice sneaked inside and then made their way by the escape route – a laboriously narrow passage that led down and out of house and grounds, emerging on the fringe of a thicket beyond the walls of the estate. It had not been an enjoyable exploit. They would have been content to make the journey once and forget it, only they had dared one another to return.

Yet today, as soon as they were into the musty little chamber, they saw that there was some change.

'He knew this could happen,' Edmund said, looking round him. 'Our father knew how it could be. He had his plans laid.'

The place had been cleared a little, and when they opened the far door on to the narrow stair, there was much improvement – one stair tread that had rotted away had been roughly repaired, the fungus had been swept from the walls. The sight of it was at once cheering and saddening. As if the dead man urged them on, as if he waved them a farewell.

'He should have been with us,' Edmund said.

Harry did not answer. He pushed into the narrow way after Edmund, and Edmund took him by the hand and led him down the stair. Then they came to the mouth of the passage and were obliged to take to their hands and knees. Even so, they were smaller than the grown men who had escaped this way ahead of them, and for them the ordeal could have been ten times worse. There was some improvement here, too. Halfway along the tunnel a shaft that had been almost blocked up had been cleared – not enough to expose it on the outside, for looking up they saw ferns lustily growing, but enough to filter in a little air and light, enough to disperse the foulness slightly.

They paused under the shaft, badly needing rest.

'Stay and breathe easy a bit,' Edmund said. His face was sweaty and his hair was sticking to his forehead, but Harry was in a worse state because he always feared the dark. In the trickle of light Edmund saw that his young brother was panting and wild-eyed. He held his face up to the thin waft of good air and gasped.

'Rest,' Edmund said. He would sooner have cried 'Hurry! Hurry!' The awful oppression of the place had hold of him and it was only with the greatest difficulty that he resisted an attempt to bolt rabbit-like towards the end of the gallery. In the gloom and the closeness he could have howled out his misery – his father gone, his home on the point of destruction, his future and Harry's utterly obscure . . .

'Best move on,' he said. 'How's it with you now?'

'Well enough.'

They began to move forward. As they did so there came a low rumbling roar behind them. The ground reverberated. Dust and dirt came raining down from the roof of the passageway. In the most acute fear he had yet known, Edmund seized Harry in his arms and tried to shield him, thinking only at that moment that the roof would come down on them and they would be entombed.

Gradually all was still again. They moved on slowly, shorter of breath even than before. Then at last ahead of them they saw the opening, a stout oak door with an iron grille, a bar securing it on the inside. The sight of it hurried them, squirming on their stomachs, over the last yards. As Edmund reached up and slid the bar and shoved the door open a foot or so, there was a second explosion from behind. This time a section of the roof a yard or so back crumbled and fell, showering them with rubble.

'Quick!' Harry cried, shrill and childish.

Edmund shoved the door harder. There was just room for him to squeeze through and drag Harry after him. They lay in the long bracken and waited, panting and terrified. Again the earth shook under them. Then they heard the great crumbling sound of a house in its death throes, chimneys toppling, walls bulging outward, roofs sinking inward – a long low rumble like a terrible groan, rolling and mourning. Then that sound ended. For an instant there was utter silence. Then other sounds began. The pattering down of small fragments that had soared high, the tinkling of glass. At last a slow and gathering crackle of fire came out of the ruins. Like some dreadful avenger it set to the task of devouring what was left of Ravenshall, that their great-grandfather had built out of a hard-won fortune, where for three generations his family and servants had lived and worked in comfortable prosperity.

Edmund had flung himself down and covered his ears, but he had not been able to shut out the sound. Now he could no longer stop his tears, and this time it was Harry who comforted him, made strong in his turn by the sadness of his brother's collapse. He put his hand on Edmund's neck, sheepishly stroking his hair, not speaking but trying in silence to rally him.

At last he did speak, and now he took Edmund by the shoulders and shook him.

'Ned! Ned! Look up, quick! Look up!'

A man had thrust aside the bracken and was gazing down at them.

'It's Barnaby!' Harry cried.

Barnaby stooped down, and without any respectful ado, pulled his master's children into his arms and embraced them.

'I do praise God!' he cried. 'Thank God Almighty for this mercy! Tell me straight – was your good father dead when you left him?'

'Aye, Barnaby. He died very quick,' Edmund answered. 'Else we'd not have come away.'

'I knew he must do so. And I did loathe myself for quitting him.'

'Why did you?' Harry asked. 'Oh why did you?'

'I give him my solemn oath to it, Master Harry – when first all the great trouble started. We did set a plot together, you might say. I swore, if he fell, however it might be, to think at once of saving his sons. That's no easy thing – leaving such a man . . .'

'Indeed, I did think it must be planned,' Edmund said. 'Him making so much stir to reach the library. And then The ten-acre, he said, And Go.'

'I am to take you to your kin, sir.'

'To Mantlemass.'

'Aye, there. He thought to tell you both the plan for safety's sake. But I think he could not get courage enough to fright you. These're cruel, hard times. God knows if we'll find our way safe. And He must guide us, for none else shall.'

'Horses,' Edmund said. 'Are there still horses?'

'Saddled ready. Done like I swore to. Lass and Dryad and little Psyche . . . And best we don't dally, Master Ned. Are you firm on your feet enough to move on?'

'Should I be other?'

'Make some haste, then. We'll ride for my sister's. She'll give us shelter till tomorrow.'

They went stealthily through the thicket. The air behind them was black and purple with great billows of smoke. Barnaby rode Lass, Edmund had Dryad; Psyche and Harry already knew and loved one another – the little nag had greeted the boy far too loudly and eagerly for Barnaby's peace of mind. For all the dreadful urgency that forced them onward, Edmund was bound, when they came to high ground, to rein in and look back. He had thrust the book inside his shirt, and now he held it, pressing it against his heart as if swearing a great oath upon it, seeing as he did so the whole of the Ravenshall lands under smoke. Not content with the house, the troopers had fired the barns and outbuildings, and even the stubble standing in the harvest fields. Though the gunpowder charges were now spent, their reverberation continued in Edmund's mind. They would remain so, he thought, beating an endless rhythm, until such time as they broke forth again into a violent conclusion. But that must come in some other place. By tomorrow or the next day, nothing would be left of the first years of Edmund Medley's life.

2

The World of Mantlemass

A man rode in to Mantlemass that winter morning bearing news no stranger than much of late – yet strange for all that and still hard to understand. It was all but eighteen months since King Charles raised his standard at Nottingham, in howling August weather; but time had made it no easier to accept that Englishman was at war with Englishman. Cecilia Highwood was sitting by the parlour window, writing in her day-book, when she saw the man crossing the court. She recognised him as one of many such fellows who collected and passed on tales of the world and the war. He would be off again after a bite and a sup for his pains, dropping in as he went at such households as might reward him for his news, riding in the day as far as Canterbury or Dover.

Cecilia rose at once, a tall, calm girl, fair-haired and strong of purpose. She went quickly out into the hall, but her older brother Nicholas was ahead of her. They met the rider at the door.

'I rid through all the miles from Midhurst, sir. Roads like iron, frost the whole way. Good roads for moving armies.'

'Are armies moved, then?' Nicholas asked. 'Last news we had, it was likely General Waller'd winter in Hampshire.'

'It's Lord Hopton's force, master. Crossed into Sussex a day past. Cavaliers, sir – and met up wi' some small Parliament force

17

north of Harting. So there come a skirmish and many left dead.'

'Then?'

'A force is left to occupy Sir William Ford's great house – Uppark, that is. And they've took back Stanstead, that's Lord Lumley's place. So the King stands the richer. And now, master, they're all snug quartered in Cowdray. There's a fine fair house, as well you may know.'

'I did see it once,' Nicholas Highwood said. 'A great house for a great family, Papist or no.'

'My mother's sister had a kitchen place there. The Castle, they call it then – for because of the great state the Montagues did keep.'

'Yes, indeed – yes, yes,' Nicholas said, impatient of such nabbling. 'So – what next?'

'*Next* is – they c'n think happy it's King's men come there for quartering. If it were t'other side, the whole treasure of the place'd be stripped and lugged off to Lunnon.'

'War's a time of bad manners. Armies find funds how they may. There's plenty fine plate melted down for the King.'

'Oh aye, for sure, sir,' said the man quickly. And he looked sideways at Nicholas. 'I took you for a King's man, master. Though why should I so?'

'Why indeed? Not every master's for the King, nor every servant for the Parliament. Easier, indeed, were it so.' He frowned. 'So we have battles back in our own countryside. Let them stay westward, I say. Last year at Chichester was near enough.'

Nicholas turned away, not liking any of what he had heard, unready to hear what more there might be. He left the man standing and went about his own affairs.

'Get you off to the kitchen,' Cecilia said to the messenger, and smiled a little, for he looked very crestfallen. 'Get your bait there as usual. Ask Giles to give your horse a munch of oats, too.'

'I only told the half, mistress,' the man said. 'Lord Hopton's set to take Arundel and hold the castle for the King. That's rightdown gospel true and no gainsaying.'

'Arundel! Miles nearer than I like to think of . . . I'll tell my brother. Now, do you get on your way and take your miseries with you.'

'I've only the telling, not the making of 'em,' he protested.

'So you have. Well, then, ask Dolly for a good cut off the ham we took down yesterday. And say I said so.' Feeling sorry for him, she fished in her pocket for a coin to give him. 'See you stop in next time you come news carrying,' she said.

She found her brother standing irresolute at the turn of the stairs, as though the news had made him uncertain even of his next daily task. She wished he had more support in his life, something better than the household hanging round his neck. She wished he would marry – and knew who it should be, but doubted that he knew as much himself.

'He says they're set to take Arundel, brother.'

Nicholas groaned. 'Not a year since Chichester and all that horror. Once Arundel's under seige there'll be bitter doings – never doubt it. Lord, lord!' Nicholas cried, 'how's a plain man to fare in such times?'

'By keeping his own counsel?'

'Easy said, hard done. I'm fairly quotted wi' the waste and pain of it – let any hear who wants, and let any who wants call me timmersome.'

'You do sound so, surelye.' His sister answered him in the country talk they had used together since childhood.

'I know it. But I must dread the day our turn come. Come it must – one side or t'other side must strike – but who's to tell of a certainty which it's to be?'

'Mantlemass is no Cowdray, Nick.'

'Mantlemass is Plashets foundry, my dear maid. Iron. Weapons. Guns. Gunstones. All. How's there to be no mighty struggle for every forge and foundry south o' Lunnon? That mean our Plashets, that bin worked for Mantlemass near one hundred year. God knoweth it's sore run down b'now. But there's water in plenty and timber still. Given men enough, we'd hear the hammers just like our grandfathers done.'

'There's no work not paid for.'

'Better times for us, you mean? Aye – but who's to pay? Which side – which Englishmen shall Mantlemass furnace-men be paid for killing?'

'Let be,' she said.

'Nay, then – tell me which you favour? Shall it be the Cavaliers, sister? Or they that's called Roundhead?'

'Do what you list, and I'll want nothing other.'

'Ah – come you and I were all the household I reckon there'd be no more than a pin to pick over between us.'

He gave her a brief, grateful smile, but he looked very tired and concerned. His responsibilities sat on shoulders not built broad enough to carry them. He had had a scholar's leaning, but hard circumstance had forced him into a different mould.

'We have our place, Nicholas,' Cecilia said gently. Loving him as she did, with so much warmth and loyalty, she hated to see him so oppressed. 'We have our land for cropping, even if it be less than once. We have the iron mill, though it be poorly served these times. We have ourselves. We have Mantlemass.'

'We have what we have only till it's took from us,' he answered. 'And whoso comes first'll do that. What days these are! What troubles for all Englishmen! Mantlemass never saw such troubles!'

She laughed at that, half to shake him out of his gloom, half to cheer herself.

'You know that's fool's talk – scholar that you are. York and Lancaster, brother – what o' those times? Tudor and Plantagenet and the rest – all the Church worries – worse than now, I'd say. Mantlemass stood then – and still Mantlemass stand. Times'll mend – now like then. And there'll *still* be Mantlemass.'

'Maybe so, maybe other,' Nicholas said, too deep in gloom to be rallied, but smiling a little all the same; his sister's passionate care for their home did often make him grin and tease her for it . . .

Cecilia went back into the parlour, returning to her writing. When she came to an end, having set down all the fresh news, she wrote: 'My brother Nicholas need great rousing from his melancholy at these events. Better indeed if he and me should say straight out which side have our prayers to win.'

Since they were so close, the silence was strange. It was her silence, too, though she knew in her heart where her sympathies were bound to lie. It was true that two hundred or so years ago, Mantlemass freehold had come as a gift from the Crown, and that Mantlemass was so dear to Cecilia that she might well have felt she owed monarchy a debt that could never be discharged.

The local stubbornness and independence of spirit, however, leant naturally towards reform and against oppression; and Mantlemass tenants and servants were all bred of the forest that gave them their nature. The King himself was lord over this forest, for it had been for centuries a royal hunting ground. A little while before the present bitter war broke over the land, His Majesty had given away to one of his nobles such rights over timber and minerals and tenantry, over iron and iron mills and the ponds and streams that served them, that few could escape a tyranny as harsh as any existing back in the wars of York and Lancaster.

'They'll never endure it,' Nicholas had said, when the new lord began setting up enclosures. He was right; the fences were torn down and burnt.

'Nor they've no need to endure it,' was what Nicholas's friend, John Verrall, had said a while later.

For by then the first tumult had come to show the meanest commoner that no authority was too high to be challenged, too strong to be put down; and this was the lesson that had come clear to Cecilia, too, not only because her tutor in this matter, John Verrall, was one she listened to with happiness . . .

Cecilia had been sitting writing a long while. The table, with drawers and cupboards to either side, had been made for her grandmother by a local craftsman – his own grandson, plying the same trade, had told Cecilia so. But he had known nothing of the secret compartment that Cecilia found only after she had been using the table for more than two years. 'The little writting tabel to my eldest grand-daughter,' Ursula Medley had instructed in her will; and so had given into Cecilia's careful loving hands all that had been harvested of the past in that place – of Mantlemass and Plashets, of properties lost in harder times, Ghylls Hatch, Strives Minnis, Tillow Holt, and one manor far into Kent that had come by marriage into the family. The years of drought and tempest and seasonal disasters, settled on the country for almost a quarter of a century, had pared away the Mantlemass inheritance.

Cecilia had never known her grandmother, but she had accepted what seemed a message across death and generations. She kept her discovery secret even from Nicholas. And would do so, she hoped with all her heart, right into the grave; for a part of what she had found in that horde of letters and papers was such heavy knowledge she dreaded it should ever be shared.

There had been years of hardship already when widowed Susan Highwood brought herself and Nicholas and Cecilia home to Mantlemass where she had been born. She and her brother, Thomas Medley, who was master of Mantlemass by then, were all who survived of their family. It was a lean and unpromising household to return to as a pensioner, as Susan found herself when her husband died. So lean and unpromising, indeed, that when Thomas Medley took a second wife, his two sons by his first marriage left home one after the other and went their separate ways. Nor, when their father died soon after, did either son return to claim Mantlemass itself or any other due. The whole burden of the household had fallen upon Nicholas Highwood. He was eighteen, responsible not only for his mother and sister, but for his uncle's second wife with her young son and daughter.

'I'm no true master here,' Nicholas often said, though he had earned the title hardly enough. 'I'm but steward. Mantlemass is my trust, not my inheritance.'

'For sure not!' his uncle Thomas's widow would reply very sharply. 'For if none other come home for it, then my son James shall be master here.'

It was a fragile claim. Jamie Medley could never be true master of his father's house and iron-mill. Long before he had reached his present nine years it had become plain to all that his wits would never be more than the wits of a troubled child.

Cecilia put away her own leather bound day-book with her grandmother's fluent, ill-spelt writings – copies of letters, with their answers; bills, tithe-lists; accounts for harvest feasting and house repairs and Christmas fare; her day-book, where she had written down all she knew of past generations, the parchment folded inside it that was an unfinished tree of the family with all its branches; another paper, older, falling into shreds, that showed Mantlemass in its first days, with only a few outbuildings, and no sign of the big Chapel Barn.

There was, too, among all these papers, one solid object. It was a key. It was tied with a tarnished gold thread to a leather tag, on which had been pricked out with a red-hot needle: *Smalle chest*.

If there were such a chest still at Mantlemass, then it could be found and opened . . . Cecilia had never sought for what more might lie locked safely away.

The fire was low, there was such a general shortage of household fuel that care had to be taken to eke out each day's supply. She must tell Giles or one of the men to stack more peat or they would never get through the winter. The weather had been hard for weeks, the frost settling in and turning the forest tracks solid and dry as bone. There was no wind. The sun shone from its slow rising to its early setting but never thawed more than an edge or so. The trees carried icicles longer than catkins.

'I've a crying in my head!' young Jamie Medley had said once to Cecilia, as the icicles tinkled together.

'Hush, then, and listen,' she had answered him.

'What is it? Oh what is it?'

'Your own soul speaking quiet, surelye.'

She saw Jamie now, as she stood by the window, blowing on her fingers. He was running fast along the track towards the house, his dog, Brave, at his heels. Jamie's mouth was wide open as if he had run so fast and so far there was no other way for him to find any breath. He would not see his cousin at this distance, and she turned away without any further thought, for he often looked wild. Besides, her mother came into the room just then to complain of the cold – and of some slight put upon her by whomsoever she happened to have in her bad books that day.

'I gave my order to that girl in the dairy, and she never so much as turned to answer. There's too little salt in the churning this last week.'

'There's too little salt, and that's the sum of it.'

'And so are servants to become lippy and insolent? They lose their manners because there's none strong enough here to be their master!'

'Mother, do hush,' said Cecilia. 'Phyllis is a good, easy girl.'

'Easy in manner, easy in virtue!'

'That's wicked talk, and you know it. Be silent, do.'

'Ah, if your good dear father were here to see me now! How I am put upon and beset! He'd never have me wear the same old gown, in-season, out-season – that he never would!'

'If my father were alive,' said Cecilia carefully, for her temper was rising, 'you and I should not be at Mantlemass, now or for these twelve years past . . . And you've four good gowns still in your closet.'

'That I have not – I have not, daughter!'

'You have the brown wool for winter.'

'Am I to wear *brown wool* like a cottager's wife?'

'A cottager's wife would think well of such a fortune!'

'Brown makes me look sallow as a quince.'

'Oh, *mother*!' Cecilia cried, and was bound to laugh.

'I should'a gone to the Highwoods for help when your poor father died – to his own people not mine . . . If I could've seen Mantlemass poor and stingy I never, never would've come running back home to my brother Medley. Poor Thomas! Poor Tom! If I'd but known how soon he was to die!'

'We'll not blame his silence on that matter, I think,' Cecilia cried, her patience leaving her. 'As for my father's family – well you know that he wed you agin them, and they never let a farthing slip between them and him after.' And she added, brutal because it was all her mother would respond to at this stage, 'Anyways, madam, it is many too many years too late to grumble!'

Then her mother sat down by the fire and wept.

'Now, mother – mother . . .'

'Such times, child – what's to be done? That this place should be so set about! Your brother tells me Plashets scarce profited at all over last year. And there's the farm all dwindled.'

'I know it.'

'How shall we live through this winter? Why do the men not work harder?'

For many reasons, Cecilia might have answered – but it had all been said before. Because there were hard times everywhere, because people had moved off to seek a better living away from the forest where they had been bred – so that cottages and hovels decayed, roofs fell in, thatch tore and sprouted. Even Mantlemass tenantry had moved away. Labour became dangerously short.

'Once, when I was child,' said Susan Highwood, 'we heard the hammers all day long, and at nights the furnaces made a red sky. There were guns and gunstones and profit in plenty.'

'There's been little need of weapons these last years, mother. There's been peace.'

'Well, that's remedied now, God knows. There's need enough now. Men need weapons to kill their brothers now – to kill even their fathers!'

'Shall we profit by it, then?'

'Why, for pity, daughter – if a man cannot buy a sword at home he'll buy it overseas! Who shall profit then?' Susan plucked at her shawl, pulling it angrily closer and tighter. 'Gentlemen are raising armies for the King, God bless him. Nicholas should set to and make them arms. There'd be honours for him, when all was over and the King safe in London, where his place is.'

Cecilia opened her mouth to answer, then closed it and shrugged. She found it wiser not to point out to her mother that here in this south-eastern part of England the tide that ran strongest ran for the Parliament . . .

'Listen!' she said, glad of an interruption. 'That's Jamie calling.'

'Ah, Jamie – Jamie! There's another burden. And little help got in bearing it from his mother!'

'Hush, now. He's upset.'

She went out quickly and met him dashing across the hall.

'I did run to and fro everyways looking for you, cousin!' the boy cried, trembling with excitement and anxiety. 'I did! I did!'

'Well, now you've found me safe. And come I'd had sense to wave from the window it'd all have been done sooner.'

'Even in the pigscot, I peered!' Jamie cried, breaking into unexpected peals of laughter.

'You'd never think to find me there, I'd hope.' She waited till his laughter subsided, holding his hand and stroking it patiently. 'Now, tell me, do, what you come to say – and why you had such a heggling time of it seeking me?'

She watched his face. He was a handsome child, only his mouth a shade slack, his eyes forever puzzling. She feared for his future and loved him not least because of his pitiful inability to care for himself. He was ever in need of cleaning up, or coaxing to his food; he had become far more her child than his lazy mother's. Now she saw as his wild untidy laughter subsided that he had forgotten what it was he had run to tell her. Well, maybe best let it go and not worry him. It was always painful to take him back over the immediate past, and she had sooner not distress him – or indeed herself by his anxious frustration. Yet something in his manner when he first called for her, in his face as she now recalled it seen from the parlour window, gave her a feeling of unease and forced her to question him.

'Jamie ran through the house and about it,' she prompted him, 'seeking, seeking. He ran down the track from the forest. By the old deer pale, was it? Was it a jump over the water? Or a quick run across the pinnold?'

'The pinnold,' said Jamie. He looked at her under his brows, worrying at the matter. He could not find what he wanted and his face began to break up curiously, the mouth twitching, the eyebrows drawing together, the eyes so wretched and puzzled it seemed they must burst with tears. Then all that changed. He shouted out in triumph 'The pinnold! The pinnold! I come across the pinnold!'

'But what before?'

Remembrance burst upon him. He clutched at her and shivered, and said very low, 'An awful thing.'

'Tell me . . .'

'A boy was lying dead in the brakes . . .'

In spite of knowing him so well, of being prepared by now for these sudden sharp horrors he would produce from nowhere to fling at her, Cecilia felt her hair rise.

'Now, Jamie, Jamie! Make sure of what you say!'

'I saw him and was frit. And Brave was frit. And we run.'

She took a deep breath. She could usually fault him on such statements – once he had said there was an old woman with white hair sitting up in the top branch of a beech tree. It was an owl, in fact, and later he claimed to have shot it with his catapult. He did sometimes claim such bold boys' antics in an attempt to keep up with the world he lived in.

'Come, then,' Cecilia said, holding out her hand. 'We'll seek him together.'

She expected him to withdraw his claim, pretending he had spoken nothing of any such matter. But watching him she knew he did not want to return to the spot. So she also knew that though there might not be a dead boy lying in the bracken, there was certainly something; for now, remembering, Jamie was very much afraid.

Cecilia pulled her cloak from behind the closet door and went out into the chill midday. Although the sun still shone, the air itself had no colour in it, and nothing moved – no animal, no bird, no branch. The boy had followed Cecilia outside, but now he was hanging back and she caught him quickly by the wrist.

'You shall show me.'

He picked at her hand on his wrist, pinching and scratching when she would not let him go, beginning to whimper. She half wished she had called his sister, Mallory, to come with them, for if he struggled too much, and she lost him, she would not know where to look for what had scared him so. The dog might lead her there, but he had run into his kennel and eyed them distantly. As she struggled across the courtyard towards the open forest, that dropped away here to the river, leaving the house proud of the lower slopes, Cecilia was all the time looking about her for help. There was none. As though swept clean by the winter chill, the house stood unattended, and all about, from the beech clump at its back to the big chapel barn with its thatch that so badly needed repair, was nothing but emptiness and quiet.

'Hurt!' moaned Jamie, pushing at her hand.

She let him go, but grabbed him by his jacket collar – and almost lost him, for it was sizes too big, an old thing left over from Nicholas's boyhood, but at the same age he had had shoulders twice as broad as Jamie's. The child began weeping quietly and sadly, and she was overcome with remorse, though she well knew he was still capable of tricking her.

'Promise you'll take me to the place, then. Promise!'

He nodded furiously, smearing at his eyes and nose. She released him as warily as she might let a bird go from her hands, expecting him to swoop away. But he leant against her, hanging on to her cloak and still crying.

'There,' she said. 'There, poor Jamie . . .' And she scooped her cloak over his shoulders and held him snug against her as they went down the slope together and crossed the pinnold, the little bridge with its turf flooring and withy handrail. On the far side the track was worn into ridged steps, and the pair of them mounted quickly. The dog had now joined them and ran silently behind, as if to avoid attention. They came to a trail through scrub, where last season's dead bracken lay felled by the frost, yet still strong and springy in its fall, hooped into shelters where birds might rest.

They went on some way, so that Cecilia began to look suspiciously at Jamie. The dog moved up and passed them, and began nosing along. Then he stopped, nose up, paw lifted. Jamie stopped, too, hanging on to Cecilia's arm, cowering under the fold of her cloak, shivering and peering into the undergrowth, then quickly hiding his eyes.

'Here, was it?'

He nodded, his teeth chattering. His obvious fear was infectious. Her own heart thudded unpleasantly and her hands had grown clammy. It would be a dead animal, she told herself – deer, strayed sheep, hog . . . But what if it should indeed be a human body lying there – and lying for how long? Her gorge rose and she swallowed with difficulty.

'Wait here, then,' she said.

Then she called the dog to go in, and followed quickly, stepping from the track into a tangle of brakes, then pausing and peering, unwilling to commit herself too far from what seemed the safety of the track.

The dog stood and whined where the russet-red bracken was flattened. She saw that what lay half-hidden was the boy Jamie had promised her.

3

Strange Kin

The boy lay face down, outstretched and still, his cheek turned against the ground, his hair a tangled mat, his boots with soles so gaping they would barely be likely to keep the frost from his toes. Cecilia crouched down beside him and forced herself to touch his shoulder. She knew at once that he was not dead, though he might very well be near to it. She tugged at his shoulders and since his bones looked sharp enough to cut their way out of his skin, he was light enough for her to turn him with not much difficulty. Certainly he was breathing, but it was a rattling business, painful to hear, and his eyes were gummed along the lashes, as if they had been closed a long time already.

Jamie had moved up cautiously and waited with his hand on Brave's collar for what would happen next.

'I did say there were a boy lying in the brakes,' he reminded her. 'I did tell so.'

'Aye, so you did.'

'A dead boy . . .?'

'Not dead. But, oh, so very particular as he is, cousin! Now – do you run home, fast, fast – faster than last time. Fetch my brother, or one of the men about the place.'

'Not dead,' said Jamie, to Brave.

'Not yet, poor mawkin – only let you and me make haste to cosset him, or he'll slip off yet. Now, run, clever child – run, come I tell you!'

'I spoke true', insisted Jamie, full of pride.

'You did, you did. Go home fast, now. Fetch any rather than none. Send them here. Then go to your mother or my mother, or your sister Mall – say get warm covers ready for the poor boy clever Jamie found.'

He stooped and kissed her cheek and then ran off, calling to his dog. She was thankfully saved the necessity of bawling at him, which sometimes was the only way to get him moving.

Then the quiet of the winter forest settled about her. The day had turned already and would not offer more than was offered now of warmth and light. A faint tawny sunshine touched the unmoving twigs of a seedling birch close by. The only movement came from a bird shifting fitfully and scratchily along dry leaves – dark and little, it was a scutty, a wren. Then it was gone and the one sound was of the boy's painful breathing, and once or twice even that seemed to have ceased. She took off her cloak and wrapped it round him as well as she could. He must be sixteen or so, she thought, for his beard was beginning though his features were still soft. He was fairish, his long draggled hair slightly curly – the hair, perhaps, of a cavalier. He was not by any means unlike her own brother in features – as she remembered him in his boyhood, in his easier years. There was a gentry look about this stranger, for all his filth, and his tattered clothes had been of good cloth. She took up one of his hands and inspected it curiously. Like the rest of him, the hand was covered with grime, besides being chapped and bleeding on the back, the fingers swollen with chilblains. For all that, it did in some curious way suggest that its owner had not been born to live by it. Considering the cold, Cecilia wondered greatly that he still lived. No doubt the dryness of the season had saved him, the dead crisp undergrowth giving him shelter. Still, he could not have lasted much longer without help, she thought. If the cold had broken and the rain had come, or if all this had happened tomorrow and not today, then he would have been lost.

Indeed, waiting, she became increasingly worried. She took back her cloak, slung it on her shoulders and fastened it at the throat.

30

imes come to me, Sarah,' Cecilia said at last, 'that we've
d there about the world by now. And how if he were
come home to Mantlemass?'
ver one of Master Thomas Medley's breed, mistress.
ons could only be babes as yet.'
t long ago – well, I did hear tell of this,' said Cecilia,
a bit as she sliced bread to crumble into the broth,
hear it someways somewhen – nay, I did read it in a
, Sarah – a letter writ long ago by my grandmother ...'
her, just,' said Sarah.
as a quarrel between brothers – three brothers – and
ent away.'
as that?'
, *long* ago,' insisted Cecilia, speaking hurriedly, still
a little, for she had meant never to speak of such
'My – my great-great-grandfather, it would have
ldest brother ... But no matter about it ... Shall we
e of the good French wine?'
said Sarah; and frowned a little as she tried to parcel
nce in time between a girl and her great-great-grand-

h smells so good I've a mind to start my supper over,'
'Sarah – I need you should teach me all your skills. I
– not near enough. If I had need – I'd choose to know
ng and baking.'
uld you ever have need, my dear creature?' cried
ng.
dmother could command her house, Sarah – I could
one day I should get left wi'out servants?'
you never shall. Not while I live.'
ust all die, Sarah. And we do live in strange, angry
nyway, I can tell you, other ladies of this house have
skilled ...'
our greatest-greatest-*greatest* grandmother, no doubt!
kills they never much knew, if I'm told right. How
b'the hour! And write, mistress! Could such dames

. . . Well, they'd fewer books, it's true. But, dear

She pulled him into shelter as she had pulled Jamie. She hugged him against her, hoping to warm him a little. She rubbed his cheeks and pinched his chin; and slapped him, though gently, for she feared roughness might finish him. A terrible anxiety filled her. She began to wonder what she should do for the best if Jamie forgot his errand and went off about his own concerns without calling help. She felt, as she held the sick boy, that she stuffed his life back into him, with great difficulty stopping up the vents by which it might drain away. She had never watched any man or any woman die, but she knew by instinct what the blue transparency beneath his eyes must mean, and the harsh texture of his dry cracked lips. She put her face against his and blew softly, as she had once seen a cow blow life into her calf ...

Then she heard someone running up the track and knew by the weight of the tread that it was a man who came. Nicholas called her name, curious, a little anxious, cautious because it was Jamie who had told a tale to fetch him from his concerns. Cecilia called back, then heard others coming, too, and knew that her worst fears were over.

Nicholas had brought Humfrey Bostel with him; and the enormously strong Ben Akehurst, who could have carried off an ox in his arms – and done so, in fact, one Lammas fair.

'Who is he?' Nicholas asked, crouching beside Cecilia. 'Did you ever see him before?'

'Never!'

'Do you know him, Humfrey? Ben?'

'Never seen till now, not by me,' said Humfrey; and Ben Akehurst echoed him.

'Well, never mind his name,' cried Cecilia, 'he's our charge, whatever he's called. And he's powerful sick, brother.'

'He moved a little ... I thought he moved. Look – look now!'

The boy shifted his head very slightly from side to side and muttered something.

'What's that he say, master?' asked Humfrey.

'Too faint to hear.'

Cecilia had heard – or so it seemed. One word, only.

'Mantlemass,' he had said, sighing it out. He opened his eyes slowly, as if great weights lay on the lids. He said again

'Mantlemass . . .' This time so clear that every one of them heard it. Then his eyes closed once more and he was silent.

By supper time three nights later, the sick boy had become a bone of contention to the older members of the household.

'Where's he from, I say? And where's he going? And how soon shall he be well enough to leave? And why must it be we who succour him?'

'Who else?' Cecilia demanded. She looked without love at her aunt Medley – Dorian, they all called her, as her husband Thomas had done, shortening the mouthful *Dorothy Ann*.

'Merely goods enough to keep ourselves – and now this stranger!'

'Should I have left him?'

'You never should have found him!' Dorian Medley cried absurdly. She could not abide anything that threatened her own comfort, which was thin enough these days. It was certain she had never forgiven her husband for dying so inconsiderately soon after their marriage. She had remained ever since in a state of indulgent self-pity that had turned her from a silly pretty woman into a sharp-mannered slattern drifting through life in a dirty-hemmed gown trimmed with torn lace. She despised and bullied her sister-in-law, Susan, quarrelled with Cecilia whenever she could, and tolerated only Nicholas – chiefly because he was the sole available masculine company. A great misfortune that she had not married again – and she thought so, too, but suitors did not come two a penny in these parts. For her own children Dorian had little use. Her daughter, Mallory, at twelve was too clever to be endured. As for soft-headed Jamie, his mother was alternately kind and cruel to him – kind when she needed him as a reassurance of the Mantlemass inheritance, cruel when he reminded her all too clearly that her only son was an idiot – and not from *her* family could the fault have come.

'Jamie found him,' Nicholas put in.

'Well, then, you see . . .' Dorian said, shrugging.

'And the only word he spoke was *Mantlemass*.'

'Why, for sure, he had been told it was the nearest good household to go begging.'

'He's no beggar, I think.'

'Then how shall we know he
And'll send his kind to take Pl

'At least,' said Susan, 'he's
You ever do moan that we're

'Aye, my good aunt, you sho
her. 'For at one blow the grov
no less than doubled!'

'How coarse you speak! Ar
shall never endure to be called

Nicholas laughed and glanc
that Dorian, when she seemed
the sake of family and sweet ch
that made them smile.

'When we know more of h
way recovered – then we shal
sharp hard times we live in.
people. Maybe they go weep

Cecilia left the rest still a
went to the kitchen. Ben A
there, with Dolly and Sue, a
swilled the dishes.

'I made a good broth,' Sa
marrow in 'em, thank the I
the rest.' Like most women
feeding up a sick man. 'Ho

'Better. And shall be bes
a finger into the broth and
'Sarah – you did see him,
a bly of my brother – do t

'Come you mention it, I
ing a ladle thoughtfully an
as she might turn a cake t
you never saw him othert

'Never.'

Sarah had known Cecil
that the girl had somethin
not question her.

'It some
kin here a
one – and

'He's ne
His grands

'Nay, bu
mumbling
'well, I did
letter, truly

'I recall

'There w
the eldest v

'When w

'Oh, long
mumbling
discoveries.
been – his e
take up som

'Best so,'
out the dista
father.

'The brot
Cecilia said.
know some
about brewi

'How sho
Sarah, smili

'My grand
not. What if

'No, no –

'But we n
times . . . A
been greatly

'Oh aye –
But you've s
you do read
do so much?

'For sure

Sarah – think on this. It's not beyond all truth I'll find myself un-lady'd one of these strange days. Do you know we have men now who say the proud and the rich should be levelled with the poor? And though God knoweth I'm neither rich nor too proud – I'm more so nor many.'

'Rest your wits, now, do,' said Sarah. 'You'll tire your poor head.'

Cecilia laughed a little. They went out of the kitchen and up the stairs, Sarah carrying the bowl of broth and a platter, Cecilia bearing the wine.

They had taken turns to sit by the bedside – all but Dorian. Her daughter, Mallory, had been happy to take her place. There she was now, as patient as a sitting bird, sustained, hours at a time, by the glorious novelty of the situation. She was twelve years old, no beauty and unlikely to grow into one, but her sharp, bright face showed where all the brains of that part of the family had gone.

'He's sleeping,' she said, rising fussily and smoothing the covers.

'Has he spoken, Mall?'

'Not a word, cousin. Nay, never a word, not even whispered. But he has looked at me and smiled,' said Mallory with satisfaction.

'Then he is better.'

'You'll not disturb him, shall you, cousin?'

'Dear Mall, he need to eat and drink and grow strong again.' Cecilia put her hand on the lad's brow and nodded. 'The fever's right out. He shall do well enough now – shan't he, Sarah? His skin's cooled a marvel, spite of the sores. His cheek felt chockly as tinder till this morning.'

They stood gazing down at him. As if he sensed their presence through whatever dreams were with him, he opened his eyes and shifted a little in the bed. He seemed to speak, but no sound came. He gave a very slight smile and tried again.

'Mantlemass,' he said. 'I was to go to Mantlemass . . .'

'Mallory,' Cecilia ordered her, 'do you run for my brother to come here. And after, go and sit with our two mothers for company. And, Sarah – best you leave me give our poor invalid his broth.'

Sarah went at once, as might be expected of her, meek from the day of her birth, made only for service. But Mallory stared and stood her ground, and flushed red with the wretchedness of being sent away now, when things looked bright.

'I waited hour on hour for him to wake . . .'

'Thanks, Mall, for your help. But go now.'

Mallory went, barely saving herself from hurling the door closed behind her.

Cecilia held the wine for the invalid, raising him up and supporting him kindly, encouraging him. He drank, and then shook his head when she urged him on.

'Where've I come to?' he asked.

'Why, to Mantlemass, my dear, as you were set to do. Now – take another sup and wait a little. Then tell what you choose.'

She watched him as he drank, and how the colour came suddenly into his face, scarred as it was with winter living and lack of nourishment. The more she looked at him, the more he reminded her of Nicholas at that age. She had tried hard enough to tell herself the idea was merely fanciful, but even speaking of it to Sarah had made it seem more reasonable. Now, watching him so closely, her mind raked back over what her grandmother's papers had revealed, that she had wanted to forget.

'It was my father made me swear to come.'

She gathered up her courage, knowing in the face of that statement that what he told her next could alter all their lives; knowing, now, that a secret once breathed can blossom into truth . . .

'Best tell me your name,' she said.

'I am Edmund Medley.'

What if Dorian had been right after all? What if she would have done better to turn away and leave him to die, and all else of the matter with him . . .

'Medley,' she repeated. 'Edmund *Medley*!'

Frail and clean and tidy now, he stared back at her hopefully.

'Come now – get this inside you,' she said, taking up the broth, delaying what must come next.

'But tell me *your* name,' he said. 'Tell me that.' But then when she told him he cried out as if he could now only despair, 'Oh then they are gone! My kin are all gone!'

'Were you to find them here?'

36

'My father said so . . .' His eyes filled and brimmed weakly with tears, and he smeared at them with the back of a swollen hand. 'I am still alone.'

'Ah, poor lad! No . . . No, forgive me. I am a Medley, too, by way of my mother. This was her brother's house. We came here long ago, when my father died.'

'My father died . . .'

He closed his eyes and muttered about troopers – about a neighbour, a Parliament man – about horses taken, his father shot, the house destroyed. All Cecilia's doubting was swallowed up in pity and sadness. She bent over him, holding his hand and stroking it, trying to reassure him and smooth away her own guilt.

'How do you come?' she asked. 'How far?'

'A long way. From Ravenshall. My home.' His eyes were now closed tight, his lips barely moving. 'Harry and I . . .'

'Harry?'

'My brother. Younger. And Barnaby, my father's true servant . . .'

He broke off, biting his lips, turning his face away from her into the pillow, as if he must bury a grief too terrible to share.

'Tell it another time,' Cecilia said, shaken.

'Dead,' he said, muffled. 'Both.'

Behind her, the door opened. She feared it might be Mallory sneaking back, but it was Nicholas. She glanced uneasily at the weeping boy, and rose to meet her brother by the door.

'Mall say you need me, sister. He's better?'

'Aye, better – but none so grig, for all that.'

'He'll not stay bethered long, not wi' you to care for him. He's young. We'll soon see him peart.'

'Nick,' she said, laying both her hands on his, 'listen careful to this strange thing: He tell me his name's Medley.'

'Medley? *Him*?'

'So he says.'

'Well, save all! The insolent devil!'

'Edmund Medley, Nicholas, from a place called Ravenshall . . . His father said he should come.'

Nicholas frowned and shook his head and stared at her.

'I see you believe what he tell . . .'

37

'Others than our uncle Thomas's sons went from home. Should they never return? Never to Mantlemass? That do seem strange to me, for this is a place should surely harvest its own. And I did think – I do think more now – he has a look of you. First-thing-ever I saw him, I thought that – just as you've our mother's colour and eyes and face shape, and she so like her brother.'

'Come out of a mould – like any running iron,' he said, and pulled his mouth down and shook his head, for it seemed hard to accept.

His bafflement caused Nicholas to stride to the bed and cry out harshly, 'Now do you wake up, whatever your true name be. Give some account of yourself.'

The boy's eyes flew open at Nicholas's tone, so hard and threatening, and he seemed to sink into the bed. Then seeing that Cecilia was still there, he rallied.

'I'll tell all,' he said, 'and gladly.' His voice had strengthened a little. 'My father said to go to Mantlemass. To your kin there, he said. Take Harry, he said, and go. He was dying . . .'

'Then?'

'Harry was my brother. We're a long time on the way – a year – more. Somewhen in summertime, Harry died. He sickened and he died. Barnaby buried him safe.'

'His father's good servant, brother,' Cecilia put in. 'What happened next?'

'Stole to feed us. Caught. Hanged.'

'Oh God save this poor world!'

'But you came on,' Nicholas said, his voice easing. 'That was brave.'

'What else would I do, sir? I had to do what my father ordered. It was his last word – his last word.' He looked at Cecilia, and his brows drew together, and all the colour he had gained left his face. 'I lost the proof of it!' he cried. 'I lost it at the last! I carried it mile on mile – I had it right through the seasons, done up in skin to keep dry. Safe tied. Right inside my shirt. Then I lost it and I can't recall how!' He caught at Cecilia's hands. 'Believe me! It was the book – the book with writing in the front – most precious and secret, my father said . . .'

'Peace now,' she said, quick and soft, as pale as he was. 'Another

38

time.' She thrust Nicholas away. 'Let him rest. Tomorrow, maybe. He's young. He'll mend fast. Only let him rest.'

She pressed her patient back on the pillow and covered him carefully.

'Your hands are shaking,' Nicholas said.

She nodded but could not look at him. She knew too much. She saw the pattern laid out clear and clean. It needed less than a quarter of what she had read in her grandmother's handwriting to make sense of all this. The book – 'most precious and secret' . . . She had already discovered there had been such a book, passed from one branch of the family to another, a long time ago. 'To heal a quarrell,' Ursula Medley had written, 'and for the sayke of truth.'

Cecilia knew what none else under that roof could know, perhaps what none else in all the living world could know. She knew that no son of her uncle Thomas could ever inherit Mantlemass – not Roger, who had gone first from home, not Simon, who had followed him; not Jamie. None of these was true heir to Mantlemass. But Edmund Medley might be.

4

Plashets Men

Riding some mornings later from Mantlemass to Plashets, Nicholas Highwood found a great deal to think about. The arrival of any stranger claiming hospitality was some cause for concern, things being at present so tight and unpromising. But much more to be thought about was the shock of hearing the lad's name. If indeed he was their true kin, then clearly he must remain as long as he wished, for his circumstances were indeed cruel. When he recovered he might very well prove sturdy – though young and thin at present, he seemed well-built. Certainly he could be no fool, for he had found his way to Mantlemass through considerable hazards, and had been about it for months, it seemed, something like a third of that time on his own. It would not displease Nicholas to have even youthful masculine support in his household of women.

'But it must be proven,' he had said to Cecilia. 'He spoke of some book he had with him . . .'

'I know of it,' Cecilia had answered.

He had been completely astounded, bitterly saddened that she had never before confided her discovery of their grandmother's papers. Nor had she wanted him to handle them, even then.

'There was a quarrel between three brothers,' she said. 'It is all here, but hard to read. Harry and Piers and Richard Medley, they were. And Harry went away and made his own place.'

'Show me the letter.'

'It is all so scambled,' she said. 'I'm set to make fair copies for you. Then you shall see how well it looks.'

'So Edmund stems from Harry? Is that right?'

'Aye – for so it is put in a family pedigree made by our grandmother – that is, she names his father, Lewis Medley. It is falling in shreds, but I shall get it all set out in time. Lewis – Piers – Harry . . . These are Medley names.'

'You tell me you know of the book he nabbled on about.'

'She sent it. She wrote so. "The book went this day back to Harry Medley's people." I read that quite clear.'

She had seemed to Nicholas to avoid his glance, and she had begun then to put the papers together, and presently slid them away out of sight, turning her back so that he never saw which drawer or cupboard held them. He frowned then and he frowned again as he thought about the business on his way to Plashets. He knew that she spoke truth about what the letters contained; he believed what she told him she had discovered, and how it made sense of Edmund's claim to kinship. What worried him still was the deep, troublesome conviction that she knew something more, and that she would not tell.

It was not so surprising that Nicholas rode that morning preoccupied and pestered. In law he was his sister's guardian, he could command her obedience and force her to hand over the letters, that he might learn for himself all that they contained. But matters had never stood between them in that manner, and he would not for worlds wish that their relationship should change. So he must be patient.

The arrival of young Edmund had forced Nicholas towards other conclusions, too. The boy had suffered severely at the hands of Parliament supporters, and he had been last year at the taking of Chichester by the Parliamentary forces, and seen what depredations followed. His sympathies could only be strongly royalist. He must be told if there were others of the household who did not share his loyalties. It now became imperative, in fact, for Nicholas to declare his own allegiance.

The ground was still hard, but the track that Nicholas rode in any case withstood all but the severest winter weather; they had laid it down years ago, with bolts of hard timber crosswise to the verge and all filled in and beaten down with slag and cinder from the furnaces. Halfway along this sound track, however, Nicholas turned aside on to less reliable ground. He rode slowly now on what he claimed as a short cut to Plashets. It took him past the Goodales' holding. Pleasance Goodale might well be about the place and pause to speak with him. Considering this, Nicholas smiled for the first time since he had set out that morning, carrying his woes and worries with him.

Since Nicholas had ridden this way most days of the week since last midsummer, and since she was as willing to speak to him as he to her, Pleasance Goodale was dawdling over feeding the chickens. He was a shade later than usual.

'A fine dry morning,' Nicholas said, pulling off his hat.

'It is so, surelye,' Pleasance agreed.

'Is your father in good health, maid?'

'I thank you.'

'At home?'

'Aye – at home,' said Pleasance. She looked up at Nicholas and struggled not to smile. 'At his prayers.'

Nicholas now dismounted. 'My sister say to tell you our hens is right out of laying. She knows you have some spell you set on yourn for winter time. I was bid ask – have you any small number to spare?'

'Spell!' cried Pleasance, with a polite shriek. 'You'll have me took up for a witch, Nicholas Highwood. Guard your tongue.'

Now she was smiling, and Nicholas's own stern, rather sad face relaxed further. Pleasance was small, brisk, round-faced, merry – but kept in order by a father whose puritanism might well have defeated the stoutest spirit.

'Well, then – no magic in it, but a certain skill,' said Nicholas. 'How shall I answer my sister?'

'That I've no great store, but better than most. That I'll happily set one by, this day, nexdy, till there's a sum worth the offering.'

'I can enquire how the bargain fare each time I pass.'

'Better I come to Mantlemass that day I've eggs enough,'

42

Pleasance said, smiling widely now, for she was beautifully without artifice. 'But it shall never be a Sunday or any such day – a fast, say. For then my father never let me stir one half of one toe.'

'They say he's took sharp against Parson Lovet at Staglye.'

'Oh for sure, I hear him wail and weep at what go on there these times. Papistical, he call it. But I know it for a fact there's naun done but to shift the communion table a foot or two!'

'Mightn't it be all men should worship how they choose?' Nicholas said, frowning.

'It might, it might! But never you let my father hear you say it. And here he come,' she added, all in the same breath, 'so do you stay as you be and face him, otherly he'll think evil of us.'

Nicholas stood his ground, therefore, until Advent Goodale drew near. Robert had been his baptismal name, but changing his way of devotion in early manhood, he had also changed his name, saying that it brought him nigher God. Nicholas was half afraid of him, half admiring. He feared his puritanism for what it might demand in others; admired his utter steadfastness, his confidence in his God, his courtesy and quiet modesty, his determination to speak out. Humble men did speak out, in this strangely shifting time, as would have seemed outside all possibility. Nor was Advent Goodale the only one among his neighbours. Others besides he had sat in church with their hats on and been reproached and upbraided from the pulpit. He was, however, the only one of them to be charged by the churchwardens and set in the stocks. There he had sat singing, not at Staglye, his own parish, where friends might have upheld him, but several miles away at Greenstead, among strangers who took their sport where they found it. A woman had thrown a crock of hot porridge at him. He still bore the mark of it on his forehead, and down one cheek where the scalding mess had stuck and trickled.

The Goodales had perked themselves up over generations of forest living. From forest guides and furnacemen, wise women and beekeepers, they had come to be Mantlemass tenantry with a good holding well maintained. Maybe they might move still further. It occurred to Nicholas, and he shifted round the thought very cautiously, for it had many corners, that Advent Goodale's grandsons might find themselves masters of Mantlemass . . .

Advent looked charitably at Nicholas, who had turned rather pale at this last thought, and greeted him mildly if firmly.

'Fair and cold, Master Highwood,' he said. 'I pray it so remain. No day, though, to stand out helving by the gate.'

'He come on a matter of eggs, father.'

'He came about your work, then. So now let him get about his own.'

'Has any come through this last three days, sir, with news from Arundel?' Nicholas asked.

'None that's good. But God and his Saints shall prevail. Parliament has great generals. And I have had word with Sir William Springett's man – his steward, John Verrall, you know him well. He come these ways raising men for Parliament – for Sir William's own regiment.'

'John's my best and oldest friend – yet I trust he stayed from Plashets,' Nicholas said, rather unguardedly. 'I've few enough to raise for myself!'

'You shall learn when you get there, no doubt.' He looked Nicholas in the eye and added, 'But I scarcely know your persuasion, sir.'

Nicholas could give no straight answer. He mumbled some farewell and went on his way, turning back once to smile at Pleasance. She seemed to have been waiting, for she raised her hand. Her tough little figure, the feet so firmly and sturdily planted, the contradictory sweep of her lashes that was no mock modesty but a kind of amused shyness, her air of courage and yet of loneliness – all touched him deeply. It was a year or more since he had known she was a maid wasted until she became a wife – six months or so since he had positively known she could be the wife for him . . . But only today, did he know with shattering certainty that he could not do without her.

Nicholas was twenty-three years old, and save for some boyish mooning he had never been in love. It hit him like an apoplexy. He shouted out loud and startled his horse into a shy. He rode on more soberly, then, his heart still thumping against his ribs, painful and pleasurable both at once. There was a foolish smile on his face that he barely contrived to straighten before coming to Plashets where he was master of men.

Nicholas had not dismounted before one of the boys came running and took the horse's head.

'Good day to 'ee, master. Sharpish, i'n't it?'

'It is so, Dicky. Tell Ben Akehurst I'm come.'

'Aye, sir; I will.'

'And, Dicky —'

Willing and cheerful, the boy paused. 'Master?'

'See Garnet get his nosebag.'

The boy slapped the horse's rump and laughed, and led him off. Nicholas heard him shout to one of his fellows that Muss' Highwood was come and wanted Ben Akehurst, and smart about it.

Nicholas stood looking about him at the crowding buildings he knew so well. A general dilapidation struck him harder than usual, because of his mood after seeing Pleasance. Smoke rose about the place, a small settlement that had once been much bigger. Workers' cottages crowded up to the head furnaceman's slightly grander dwelling. At one time, the foundry's master had lived on the site, but that house was now fallen, its remnants used to shelter pigs and goats. There was no furnace blowing, but the forge was working. They were making shares and crooks, scythes and sickles, nails and bolts and shoes; also fine hinges for oaken doors, made on designs that were traditional there, all stamped with the trademark, the Plashet Lily. Such things sold very far afield, but Nicholas that day found himself weighing them against what had been in the making there in his grandfather's day. Spain was threatening, then, and they had bored cannon at Plashets. They had made gunstones and pikeheads, flintlocks, the still valued crossbow and all tackle needed for maintenance. Long before that, other iron mills than Plashets had been at work on arrows, on great swords.

The days of war, even the later days of threats of war and invasion, had been prosperous days. Prosperity offered comfort, but if it came now it must come because Englishmen needed to drive back and slaughter their fellows. Nicholas, whose nature was almost unfortunately mild, preferred the peaceful goods his people forged for him; yet he bitterly resented the decline of Plashets, finding no comfort in the fact that circumstances had caused the decline, too, of many a neighbour. He knew he bore the wrong name for that place. He should have been a Medley – the son of a

45

son, not of a daughter. He blamed the break in tradition for what Plashets had become, telling himself he could have beaten even the shortage of timber had he been a stronger man, one born and bred up on the forest.

Dicky came running back.

'A man come up an hour past, master, talk's a lot. Ben's hooked fast as shingled mine, sir!'

'What man's that? What's his business?'

'I take him to be come about shoeing, sir. Ben's in the forge when he come, but bobbed out drackly he see'm. And stuck fast ever since.'

'Where are they?'

But then he heard voices, and saw a whole knot of men over near the head of the pond. A well-dressed stranger was leaning in a casual, friendly way on the shafts of a cart. Dicky had been right to say that Ben was caught as on a shingling tool, for each time he moved away the stranger grabbed him mockingly by the bib of his leather apron and hauled him back.

'Wait, now!' Nicholas heard him say, laughing. 'You shall wait!'

'Nay, now, sir –' Ben cried, shuffling sideways, putting the hand away and casting quick, anxious glances in Nicholas's direction.

'And *Nay* to you, man – for you shall listen!'

Ben Akehurst, enormous man that he was, seemed too courteous, or perhaps too awed by the man's good clothes and fine horse, to give him one shove and so escape. Then he saw Nicholas approaching, and this brought him strength. He plucked himself from the stranger's hold and advanced towards his master, his face as ever open, simple, devoted.

'Who's this?' Nicholas asked.

'Come from the Earl, master. A new man. Bailiff, or some such – I doubt he knows his duties. No countryman, surelye.'

'But why's he here, Ben?'

'He come for help, Mus' Highwood, so he tell. Seeking help o' Plashets. His words, sir.'

'Help? What help?' Nicholas did not wait for any answer, since he knew what it must be. His lordship, so recent a beneficiary of the King – what help should he seek but arms?

46

'Guns, Ben?' he said softly. 'Guns and gunstones?'

'Aye, that. He spoke out in a fine stodge.' Ben looked at Nicholas and frowned. 'Shall you come talk with him?'

'Let him come to me,' Nicholas said, staring at the stranger across the intervening space.

The man did turn at last to see where all the rest were now looking so uneasily. But he remained with his elbow on the shaft, eyeing Nicholas slowly. In fact, each measured the other, chin to toe, eyes to crown, and for some seconds neither man moved.

Then one of the Plashets men, Sam Hoath, shifted his feet and cleared his throat, moving towards Nicholas, and saying at the same time, somewhat urgently to the visitor, 'Sir! Sir – Master Bailiff, sir . . . Here's Mus' Nicholas Highwood of Mantlemass and Plashets.' Then he said to Nicholas, 'Master – Ben'll have told you – here's his Lordship's own bailiff. So he tell,' he added, rather subtly; and having completed a courteous task, stepped back looking very relieved.

His lordship's bailiff straightened up at last. He moved enough towards Nicholas for Nicholas to move in his turn and still feel that dignity could be satisfied.

'Stapley,' the man said, bowing. 'Henry Stapley, Master Highwood of Mantlemass – and Plashets.'

'Stapley of Lewes?' Nicholas asked, thrusting in his turn, for there was not much royalist feeling in that town.

'Never! I am a gentleman, sir – no ranter of Lewes, or any other damn town in these parts. My master being a Lord, and his master being the King – so by declension I am bound to be his Majesty's man.'

'And so – ?'

'And so I am come to batten on your loyalty, sir.'

'How shall you do so?' Nicholas asked cautiously.

'He come to curmudgeon for guns, master,' Humfrey Bostel said, shouldering a little forward – meaning he had come to drive a hard bargain.

Stapley laughed at the wording. He spoke himself with the sharper, uglier tones of a city man. 'Here is why I come to *curmudgeon*. I have been instructing your fellows in the news. The Cavaliers are marching to take Arundel, to invest the castle and hold it

47

for the King. But the treacherous Parliament must strike back, or else we are not at war! So my master calls for supplies. Not only guns – horseshoes – nails.'

'For *Arundel*? There's a-plenty smiths more handy.'

'And a-plenty disaffection among such commons, too,' said Stapley wryly. 'And my lord sooner sends by the cartload off his own territory for his own regiment.'

'His own territory?'

'Come now, come. You know who is given rights over you here. If he choose to raise his own regiment, along with other loyal nobles, he will call on his own people. And so he calls for arms on his own ground, over which he has rights of mineral and labour, too.'

'No rights over Plashets, Mr Stapley, as being part of the manor of Mantlemass. So – no rights over Plashets men.' Nicholas spoke mildly, but he saw and felt his Plashets men shift and straighten, and knew for the first time how closely they had been watching and listening. 'You will know, Mr Stapley, as being bailiff to his Lordship, that Mantlemass lie outside his land. It come to my family a free gift from the Crown.'

'Well,' said Stapley, easily enough, 'you shall show me your title and then we'll see. Best bring it to my house tomorrow or the next day.'

'No,' said Nicholas.

'No?'

'You have my word. I've told you my title. The gift was made in old King Harry's time. Some generations gone – as you'll be well able to calculate.'

'And because of it, the Crown commands your loyalty! Good – ah very good indeed. So then let's say the order's given and taken.'

'Say as you please.'

'And none so curmudgeonly, either. At a fair price that his lordship shall hit upon. So – good-day to you.'

He turned sharp and swift on this declaration, feeling the advantage to be in his hands, no doubt, untied his horse and vaulted showily into the saddle. He almost overshot, and swayed, and grabbed at the creature's mane, so that it tossed its head in protest and nearly caught him on the chin. Somebody among those watching gave a loud gruff laugh, then stifled it in a cough every bit as insulting. Then horse and rider swung away.

The four or five men around Nicholas stood silent. They were watching him and he knew it, and knew that now he had indeed to make some declaration. They had approved his stand, and the choice he had so long delayed had all but been made for him.

'I never did yet declare myself,' he said slowly. 'Not here, nor any other place. We've not spoke together any time, which way we see the wind blow for us.'

'Master, we know our own thoughts, each and every,' Jim Bostel, Humfrey's brother, answered. He was a man handy at both forge and furnace. It was known though no longer spoken of, that Bostels had a family connection with Medleys, back many generations. 'And now, sir, it mun be said, too, that the young lads know theirn. There's Martin Grover and two o' Nick Hendall's sons gone off.'

'Gone off, Jim?'

'To Colonel Morley of Glynde, sir. There's a rareish to-do been made of his recruiting. So off they three boys did set. I did tell 'em I dunnamany times to think on it. It's life and death, I tell 'em, but the young don't see beyond today. They would go dupping off to fight for the Parliament.'

This was bad news for an ironmaster short of labour, and yet Nicholas stirred a little at the lads' quick answer to a call so old as the call to battle. He half envied them the freedom to come and go – a freedom not his own.

'They've naun to say good of the King, then?' he said.

Bostel cleared his throat and straightened his shoulders a bit, though they hardly needed it, and answered steadily 'Naun. And all us here, Master Nicholas, having spoke together do know our own minds on this.'

'Best speak out, then.'

'Sir. Come there's work took over for his lordship of the Manor, it'll not get done by Plashets men.'

Ben Akehurst moved at that as if he would quiet Bostel and those others who had quickly murmured in his support. He looked anxiously at Nicholas. He was the gentlest among them, though he could bend cold iron if he was set to it. He would not lightly

49

offend any he respected, and he had seen Nicholas grow up and change with the weight of his responsibilities, and knew his difficulties.

'Shall you speak out to us in turn, master?' he asked quietly.

Nicholas hesitated a second only. The knot of men had been increased by others moving up to listen, but those in the forefront he had known since childhood. They had worked for his uncle Thomas, and some of them remembered his grandfather. Hoath and Bostel, Akehurst, Thomsett, Hendall and Henty – such names had served Mantlemass before Medleys followed Mallorys and began to work iron. Nicholas knew how much he wanted their sons to know his sons. He felt a great surge of warmth for them, not only for themselves, but because they had hauled his conscience on trial before them, and now he was forced to a decision long overdue . . .

'We think and shall act alike,' he said. 'You give me your thoughts straight-out. There's mine.'

They shifted, exchanged glances, began to smile.

'But we'll get to forging shoes and nails, bolts and gun shot,' Nicholas said. 'And come Master Stapley ride this way about his lordship's business, and do enquire of any one of you – give him his answer one way, t'other way. For there'll be others of a different turn of mind'll need supplying.'

Now indeed they were smiling. There was something in their rough, tough manner he had not quite seen before. They had never been anything but loyal. It had been his burden to believe that loyalty was in fact less to himself than to the memory of his uncle Thomas. Before his eyes he saw the change set in. They moved towards him, as if impelled forward. By chance he was standing on ground a little sloping, so that he had the advantage of them, looked down on them. For a moment he felt like a leader, he half expected his men to bend a knee and vow allegiance. The strange impression troubled him, for had it not been said by now that men should be levelled, one to another? And had he not placed himself on the side of reform?

He stepped down the slope, refusing his advantage. He held out his hand to Ben Akehurst, and Ben with an age-old gesture wiped his palm on his thigh, then clasped the offered hand. The rest moved in behind him, their hands outstretched in turn, a kind of fervour in their eyes; and Nicholas held two at a time of these hard, dark-skinned, scorched hands, and pressed and wrung them. An extraordinary feeling of strength, of goodness moved him. His spirit matched theirs. They were at one as they should have been long before this.

'God judges all,' he said. 'Trust him to uphold the right . . . But we must labour to win, surelye.'

'Amen to that, master!'

'Work at Plashets sunk so low these last years, I wonder, time and often, how we do sustain ourselves.'

'There's plenty ore yet, Mus' Highwood. Plenty to be dug and roast. And a mortacious great horde o' stuff ready forged might serve still. Plashet-forged, my grandfather'd say,' Henty claimed, bringing out once more a story so old that Nicholas smiled and the rest laughed and nudged one another. 'My own grandfather did just recall Master Richard Medley. A rare great man, sir – a rare man for iron, he was. My grandfather never forgot'm, though he were a tiny boy when Mus' Richard died.'

'I hear tell he was a great man,' Nicholas agreed.

'Aye, though he were born crooked i' the shoulder – and not the first nor last Medley shaped so.'

'Aye, no doubt, no doubt . . . But let's think, now, what's best. Get indoors, Ben – and Sam Hoath and Humfry – all the timber men first. There's a plenty young stuff, too young. We'll need to fell wisely . . .'

So then they began to move back towards the mill, talking together, slapping one another on the back. For a great day had come, with master and men of a mind together, strong and purposeful.

'And some say that Richard Medley got named for the crooked old king,' Henty was gossiping on. 'Like my own good wife got christened Elizabeth, to honour the old Queen.'

'There'll be new names, come there's no kings,' said someone.

It was after dark when Nicholas returned home. He was tired but still exultant. He had found himself praying for strength as he rode, and now he was confident that he would receive it. Today's events, too, had somehow made all his hopes of Pleasance Goodale stronger and nearer.

Coming into the hall, glad to think of pulling off his boots, he heard voices in the parlour.

'Who come calling, Giles?' he asked the man who had greeted him at the door.

Giles was a taciturn, small man, rusty-haired and with the long-lipped look common thereabouts. He was self-appointed as Nicholas's personal servant, rode with him whenever he could, and much disliked and disapproved his going unattended even as far as Plashets.

'It's Mr Verrall, sir,' he answered, taking Nicholas's hat and cloak.

'Has he been long?'

'He come not much after noon. Set and sure to speak wi' you. Bin wi' the ladies in the parlour since dinner time.'

John Verrall and Nicholas had been friends since boyhood, sharing schooling and sport, dreaming of going together to the university in Oxford. For Nicholas the hope had never had much chance of fulfilment. But John had patrons in the Springett family, his grandfather and his father had both spent a lifetime in their service. So it was with young Sir William Springett that John shared his student days, learning from him to love the cause of freedom. He remained in Sir William's service, administering those family lands that bordered the upper Ouse to westward, the Cuckmere on the east. He rode the few miles to Mantlemass as often as he might, but too seldom to please Nicholas – or, he believed, his sister.

'Good that he come, Giles. He'll most like stay overnight – so tell Sarah, if my sister not done so.'

At that moment a great noise and shouting broke out beyond the closed parlour door – and it was certainly not John Verrall's quiet voice that was raised.

The sound sent Nicholas striding across the hall as if to forestall some disaster. But he knew as he thrust open the parlour door that he was already too late. The boy, Edmund Medley, was on his feet, and Nicholas had a quick impression of the women's faces, shocked and pale.

'I was at Chichester!' Edmund was shouting, if shouting it could be called, for his voice was hoarse and weak, though it was furious enough. 'I know, I tell you! I saw! There were innocent people murdered and dying – the townsfolk had their roofs blasted away above them! There was blood in the streets – blood – blood in the streets! Leave me – let go!' he cried, as Cecilia tried to catch his arm in some attempt to quiet him. 'The cathedral,' he rushed on. 'You know well what they did to the cathedral – you've heard of that? But I saw it! How the troopers did storm in and none stayed them – their generals stood by. They rode their horses up to the very altar, and all over the dead lying there for centuries was dung and filth! They hacked and tore and defiled!'

'Oh hush!' cried Susan Highwood. 'God save all! Oh do hush, child!'

Dorian Medley at this moment sprang to her feet, and her shabby gown caught in the arm of her chair and tore some inches more. 'Long live the King!' she cried, very shrill. 'God save his Majesty! You hear, Mr Verrall? We all are loyal subjects of King Charles in this house – all – all! And you shall take that news to your masters, the Springetts. All here hold allegiance to the Crown!'

Nicholas did not hear what Verrall answered, if indeed he replied at all, for he stood looking diffident and embarrassed. If he did speak, his words were drowned by Cecilia's furious voice.

'Speak for yourself, my good aunt Dorian! Speak for yourself as you choose – but never for me! I pray you, never speak for me what I hold to or what I deny!'

At the end of a day already deeply portentous Nicholas knew that the war had suddenly come close. It had moved into his own home and could split his hearth in two.

5

Arms for Arundel

They were so occupied with their own quarrel that they none of them saw Nicholas come in.

'Why, dear God in Heaven!' Dorian Medley cried. 'Am I to say I have a niece sworn to Cromwell? Am I so?' She swung round and seemed to bear down on her sister-in-law, Susan. Anger suited Dorian, her fine eyes flashed and all her lassitude left her. 'This is your doing, madam!' she cried, leaning over Susan as if she might hammer her with her closed fists. 'You ever did let your daughter say and think as she felt fit! Now see what we are come to!'

'Let be, let be!' poor Susan protested. 'How should you and yours fare, save for what my son Nicholas has ever done to keep us all fed and clothed?'

'And do you tell me he's o' the same persuasion? Do you so? And all this long year and longer, with such battles and such misery, have you let me live here in ignorance of his wickedness? Am I to see my poor innocent children corrupted and disloyal?'

'Persuasion? Corruption?' Susan shrilled. 'I know nothing of them. I only know what we have all known here – the wisdom to keep our own counsel. And I have thanked God for it – that we live out of the world enough to keep free of strife! Let them fight in the west, if they choose – and in London and about Oxford and in all the North – but let us keep our peace. Let us keep it, I say! Else shall all our life be blackened and miseried and none among us trust brother or cousin, child or servant, and all shall run blood and disaster and no help for any of us to live quiet in mind again!'

'Oh, my dear good mother!' Cecilia cried, half sorrowing, half laughing at the vehemence that left Susan leaning back, panting, in her chair. 'I never heard you speak so much, nor so sturdy in all my life! And you have changed your tune a little, I think.'

But this only made her mother burst into great sobs and thrust her way from the room. She almost knocked over Nicholas as she went.

'Speak to them!' she cried.

'The poor fool,' said Dorian, straightening her tattered ruffles.

'And what battle shall this be called?' Nicholas asked, so quiet and unmoving, yet so forceful that Dorian flounced into her chair, and Cecilia flushed. 'Shall it be called the battle of Mantlemass? Or the battle of Highwood and Medley?' He looked at Edmund, who still stood clutching the back of his chair. 'Was it you – cousin? Was it you set all this on? A poor way to pay a debt – I am bound to say it.'

'Best blame me, friend,' John Verrall said quietly. 'I came here upon business for my master, Sir William Springett. I did speak of how he raised his regiment. Eight hundred men, and never a beat of the drum to call 'em. As I guess, the young gentleman took me for a recruiting sergeant – and spoke out hard against the Parliament.'

'As I have cause!' cried Edmund, his voice increasingly wavering and weak. 'As I have great cause!'

'Sit down,' Cecilia said, and pressed him back into his chair. She had set him by the hearth with cushions and a coverlet for his knees. 'Now rest, do, Edmund Medley. I never should've let you from your bed so soon.' She put her hand on his forehead, then drew the covering closer round him. 'Keep the healing snug. I wanted you warm by the fire. Since you act so sprackish, you'd be safer away in your bed.'

'I'm well enough here,' the boy muttered, shaken and ungracious.

'I pray Mr Verrall may pardon you, cousin.'

Dorian broke in – 'Mr Verrall brings shocking news of Arundel, nephew Nicholas. The town beseiged – the town taken – the castle held . . . I know not what more!'

'Is it so?' Nicholas asked Verrall.

'Lord Hopton took the town for the King, and has left the castle garrisoned. Sir Edward Ford in command – at least, I hear that to be so. There's a great threat to the people of the town – townsfolk must ever bear the brunt. Sir William Waller's on the march out of London – he went for men and arms, they say, and has what he sought. A good force, Nicholas – a very useful body of horse and foot, both.'

'So then there must be great bloodshed . . .'

'Aye – I do fear so. And my commission must be for all aid – for men and arms. For though my master has dwelt lately in Kent – this is his country and here's his true home where his heart lieth. So, as I see it, sir, many men and lads of this wealden countryside must die. And how many of 'em truly knowing why?'

Because he spoke so quietly and so bluntly his words brought straight to Cecilia's ears the very sound of clattered steel and thudding gunfire; and the smell, sweet and sickening, of blood and wounds and corruption, of cruel and lonely death. There were three there in the room with her, any one of whom might so die, and the thought of it made her feel sick and faint. She, too, had had a coward's hope that she might never need to declare herself. The town of Arundel, set so sweetly above the river, its castle like a crown upon the hill, was suddenly a neighbour. If she judged her brother right, arms would go from Plashets to sustain the conflict there. It was inevitable and right – but because of it destruction might come to all of them. In such times as these, even Mantlemass could fall.

By the second week in that December the frost still held, the weather was cold and clear. It was a little more than a week since Nicholas had ranged himself with his men. It had been very satisfying that he could also range himself with his friend.

'Only today,' he had told John Verrall, 'the men did remind me of much stored armament. It shall set the whole matter in motion.'

'Aye – but see we get no rusty weapons! Men have gone into

these late battles with their grandfather's swords and little sharper! Our men deserve better.'

'And shall have better, too. But there's much can help of the old stuff – and you can trust Plashets not to send the Lily out to be dishonoured!'

'God bless you, friend,' said John. 'I shall have good news for Sir William.'

It was on the Tuesday after this exchange that young Edmund Medley was strong enough to walk out into the cold air at last. Mallory was set to mind him and took her commission seriously.

'Now do you just doddle a pace or two – and mindfully,' she ordered, 'then do you rest a little.'

'I'm not into my grave yet,' he answered, almost snarling it in the despairing ill-temper of convalescence.

'And I'm to see you stay clear of it,' she snapped back. 'So – come you decide to kill yourself, pray set down first in good cold writing that the trouble were none o' my making.'

'Where was I found – that day?' he demanded. 'That's where I'll go. Take me there.'

'Too far, surelye.'

'Then – do you shove yourself off and I'll find it alone.'

'Nay I will not. And you shall not.'

He kicked out at a stone in his fury.

'Best take my arm,' she said officiously. 'I see you're took swimey and may fall.'

'Swimey! There's a word!'

'Good Christians use it hereabouts.'

'Get to the devil, then,' cried Edmund, hating all about him.

The trees were held motionless against a pale, unclouded sky. Yet there had been a slight thaw overnight, bringing a powdering of snow that was decked very delicately over the remnants of autumn – the russet, bowed bracken, the few berries the hard-pressed birds had left – for tomorrow, Mallory said. Though the air was crystal clear near at hand, the slightest gathering of mist over the far hills did speak of change. Mallory took her companion down the shallowly sloping track towards the little river that was the Mantlemass boundary to south and west. There was a fallen treetrunk lying in a hollow there, and the sun shone quite warmly in this sheltered place. Mallory sat down and ordered Edmund to do the same.

'If I choose,' he said.

'Pray choose, then, for any and all's sake, Edmund Medley. For if you're to mend you must rest. And if you so mend then your temper may mend, too. For which I'd praise heaven.'

Grudgingly he sat down, and grudgingly forced himself to a faint grin.

'We all do long for you well and happy,' Mallory got in quickly, before his mood could blacken again. 'We do – we do!'

Edmund said, very low, 'I am a sad trouble to all at Mantlemass.'

'Who ever say so? For sure it's a baddish time for visitors. It was a poor, mouldy crop – little enough left to feed the beasts, so you'll get scant meat and none by springtime. No matter. We'll be scant together. Anyways – how should any Medley turn other Medley from the door?' She looked at him rather severely. 'As well my cousin Cecilia is a good scholar and could read in the letters and such that our grandmother left behind her.'

'I know it,' he said soberly. 'There it was all writ down – that my father Lewis Medley was grandson to Harry Medley of Ravenshall, own brother to Piers Medley of Mantlemass. And who was he, if not your father's grandfather?'

Mallory exploded into laughter. 'Lord, cousin – aye, I'll believe and call you cousin – how you have it off all pat as a prayer!'

'So might you – if all the kin you know had come to be names on a paper. So, good Mall, take me where they found me. I put the book safe somewhere. Why not there?'

Mallory did not answer immediately. The day after he came to his senses he had begun nabbling about 'the book', and by now she was ready to believe it had existed. But it did not greatly matter to her whether Edmund were her kin or not, so long as he remained at Mantlemass. She had never had anyone of her own generation to talk to. Edmund was a few years her senior, but girls, she thought comfortably, are ever older and more sensible for their years than boys.

'I'll take you when you're stronger. I promise it straight and solemn,' she said.

'I was sick and I put it from me – I put it where it should be

58

safe. My father said I must bring it to Mantlemass, and so, somehow I must. It'll tell over again what Cecilia found out,' he insisted.

He was getting rather wild and distressed. Mallory pulled him to his feet and began to urge him back towards the house, for Cecilia would never forgive her if he had a return of fever.

'Now I have it planned,' she told him. 'Jamie shall find your book for you. Jamie's short of sense but he have a nose for finding.'

As if she had summoned him, Jamie came at that moment from over at the far side of the house, where the farm was, with so many of its buildings half in ruin. His dog was at his heels, but when he saw Mallory and Edmund, Jamie perversely ran in the opposite direction. Mallory let out a piercing, unmaidenly whistle, and both dog and boy halted as sharply as if they had been jerked by some string she held in her hand. Then Jamie turned and came reluctantly towards his sister.

'He's sadly dim,' Edmund said.

'There's many worse. There's a fault in every generation, so my father tell me once. Like a stammer – my brother Simon – my half brother that went away – he stammers powerfully. Or sometimes a crooked bit in the back – '

'Well, there!' cried Edmund. 'I had an aunt so!'

Jamie came up to Mallory slowly, then shoved his head against her arm as if he truly loved her.

'Edmund and me have a task for you, Jamie. Come you and Brave found him lying in the brakes, he left a book behind. Now I do hope you may look for it, and bring it him, and he'll give you . . . What can you give Jamie for his pains, cousin?'

'Nothing. For I have nothing,' he answered roughly.

'Well, then, I shall find something for you,' his sister told him. 'And see you bring it me straight – no hiding of it in your treasure hole.' Jamie flushed furiously and scowled. 'He keep his treasures hid, Edmund. And I know where, too. And once I looked. He did weep and wail and kick at me. And that put Cecilia in a black rage wi' me for setting him on . . . Shall I tell Edmund where the treasure hole is, Jamie?'

'Stop baiting him!' Edmund cried; and looked glad when she reddened.

By this time he was trudging the last steps to the house, and she took fright and dragged him along and shoved him in over the threshold.

'Go by the fire,' she ordered him. 'Sit quiet as a socklamb till I fetch what'll warm you.'

She ran to the kitchen to beg Sarah for a cup of spiced ale for the invalid. It was tiresome to find Cecilia there; she and Sarah had long been comfortable gossips together. 'Nabbling with the servants,' Mallory's own mother called it, looking down her fine nose. Mallory had to stand waiting for a space in the conversation, as Sarah and Cecilia decided whether to take flour for a crusted pie that day, or save it for another.

'Oh, let it be today!' Cecilia cried at last. 'And take some pigeons, Sarah, while they're brave and plump. It's too easy to spare 'em till they're ribby and not worth the plucking.'

'We'll all be ribby, come spring,' said Sarah. 'The whole world come ribby these days, mistress.'

'What is it, Mallory?' Cecilia asked at last.

'Edmund's took a shade particular, cousin. Shall Sarah spice him some ale?'

'Sarah shall show you the way,' Cecilia corrected her. 'You and me and all others in this house had best learn to use our own hands. If the war go for Parliament they say there'll be none servant and none master, but all level. So ladies must learn to be women!'

'Who tell such a tale?'

'Mr Verrall, for one,' said Cecilia, turning to count through the apples Sarah had brought from the storeroom.

Mallory shot a glance at Sarah, and Sarah was busy setting out cinnamon and nutmeg for the spiced ale.

'Mr Verrall talks a lot,' said Mallory.

'A lot of sense, maybe, Mall.'

'Well if it's to be so,' Mallory cried, 'then I'll wed with a ship's brave captain, and sail to the New World, and make Mantlemass over again – but I'll be mistress of servants, see if I'm not.'

'Did I tell you,' said Sarah to Cecilia, 'what Dan Grover told my good man? How three brothers o' hisn are gone there? Took ship from Plymouth, he say, and bound for Virginia.'

'Oh, I do recall how they come here, all three, seeking work. My own brother felt great shame to turn them away. How does a man live, far from his own?'

'And all among savages, among wild beasts – so they tell it. But there, mistress, they was all stived-up at home, wi' nine straight christened, and two chance-born. Poor Bet Grover! I doubt she'll know if to howl or huzzah to see 'em go!'

The kitchen was warm, the gossip pleasant. Far from its comfort men rode a hard bitter countryside, seeking battle, and half of them, perhaps, not knowing why. Cecilia watched Sarah help Mallory prepare Edmund's drink, but her mind moved beyond and away from the small domesticity. She had been deeply disturbed by the tale Edmund told, of his own home burned, of his father dying, of the awful scenes he had witnessed, being in Chichester when Waller took the city from the Royalists and let his soldiers run loose to burst upon the great cathedral. How she hated what she heard of the destruction then – of the hacking and defiling, of a soldier pricking out with his sword the painted eyes of King Edward VI's portrait hanging among those of the other kings of England, and crying out that all abuses stemmed from him and his prayerbook. It was easy enough to understand the simple revolt against the King's attitude towards Parliament over the years. Such matters did lead to rebellion, always had and always would, no doubt. This was a plain black and white business and no further adornments were needed in the matter of taking sides. The increasing religious fanaticism running side by side with the cut and thrust of battle was far harder to swallow. Cecilia sincerely praised God, as she had been brought up to do; but the niceties of ceremony or the lack of it, the fear and hatred of popery, the pernicketing over the use of one word or another, the hatred of show – even of music and singing that did so uplift the spirit – puzzled and confused her. The bitterness displayed at the parish church, the near hatred of the exchanges between Advent Goodale and Parson Lovet had indeed been very frightening. Cecilia would not forget Pleasance's white face as the churchwardens dragged her father from the church. Yet both Mr Lovet and his adversary were mild, kind men in their own way of life.

The ale was ready, and Mallory carried it to the parlour. Cecilia went with her and heated the clean iron, but let Mallory thrust it to sizzle in the mug.

'Now drink it down, cousin,' she said, handing it to Edmund. 'You never tasted better, for I prepared it my very self.'

Cecilia laughed, but she was happy to see them together, to see Mallory with some concern more than her own restricted routine – for she was ordinarily little more than her mother's unwilling handmaiden. The new interest had improved her temper and even her looks.

Another week, and Edmund was walking on his own. His mood had lifted and he was full of gratitude, and full of doubts how he should repay what had been done for him. They had accepted him as one of them. He had told all he knew of his own branch of the family, sometimes confirming what Cecilia knew from her grandmother's letters, sometimes filling in what had happened since, so that she wrote it down carefully. One day, she said, she would have it all fair and clear to see, a great tree of Medleys and Mallorys right back to that first owner of Mantlemass, who had willed the house to her niece's husband, Lewis Mallory. But though they all urged Cecilia to set about the business, she put it off, nor would she let any single paper of her grandmother's out of her hands, but kept all hidden, secret even from her brother, who was patient almost beyond reason, so Edmund thought.

The moment he was able to sneak out of the house without Mallory following, Edmund went searching for what he had lost that none had been able to find; the book entrusted to him by his father, that he was to return to Mantlemass as proof of his identity. Cecilia could confirm that the book had gone from Mantlemass to Ravenshall, but she seemed unable to say why. Something to do with mending that quarrel between three brothers . . . In a way, the book itself was no longer needed. Yet it was so important to Edmund to recover it that he almost felt he would retrace his steps, if need be, right back to the last moment he had positively handled the carefully wrapped packet. Only, because of the confusion of his collapse and his illness, he could not remember when that had been.

'Show me where you did find me lying,' he ordered Jamie. And Jamie took him to the place and watched solemnly as he trampled the brakes round about, and crawled in under the bramble bushes seeking what he had lost.

'Shall it be treasure you find?' asked Jamie. 'Gold?'

'You know well what I'm looking for, cousin James,' said Edmund severely. 'For you were set to look for it yourself, long before this. And much good that did.'

'James!' shouted the boy, overcome with mirth at this formality, and flinging himself down on the frosty ground to writhe with laughter.

'Peace!' cried Edmund, sourly. He sat back on his heels and tried to think. They were high up the track from the river, and across the bottom, through the leafless trees, Mantlemass stood quiet enough, though behind and to the far left of the building there was some activity at the farm.

'There she go,' said Jamie suddenly, very low.

'Who, pray?'

'My mother.'

Sure enough, along the sheltered river back, Dorian was walking rather quickly, looking neither to left nor to right. A few seconds carried her out of sight.

By this time, to his annoyance, Edmund was feeling foolishly weary. He said they should go home. They had almost reached the house when something sly in Jamie's voice as he said *There she go* echoed in Edmund's mind.

'Where was she going?' he asked, catching the child by one wrist.

Jamie looked wild, and twisted so sharply Edmund had to let him go and grab at his own wrenched wrist. Jamie dashed ahead and into the house by a side door. Edmund followed slowly, dragging his feet but not willing to admit how tired he felt. At this hour of the day, Cecilia would most likely be in the little upstairs parlour, the solar of the house in its early days. He pulled himself up the stairway, hanging on to the banister rail and panting slightly.

'I shall have no sympathy for you,' Cecilia said. 'I know how far you have been.'

Jamie had reached her ahead of Edmund and had clearly enough told his own tale. Only she had no time to rebuke him any further, for one of the servants came scurrying to say the master was wanted in the hall, where he had a caller.

'She do mean *Nicholas*!' cried Jamie, as if he had realised for the very first time that Nicholas and 'the master' were one. 'I know who come,' he said, as the maid ran off to continue the search. 'I see him ride in as I come up by the little stair.'

'Who, then?' Cecilia asked, taking his hand to calm him, for he was jigging with exictement at this very ordinary event.

He tugged at her arm, standing on tiptoe so that he could speak close to her ear. Then he pulled back to watch her face.

For a second she looked startled almost as far out of her wits as he was . . . Then she pushed him away sharply, so that at once he broke into crying.

'Oh hush!' She tugged him back to her again and kissed him. 'I meant naun cruel, my dawlin.'

She went out of the room, crying 'I'll find Nicholas,' leaving Edmund to wonder why she had turned so red. 'The one you look for,' was what Jamie had said. She knew who he meant and that what he said was true, only she had not faced the fact roundly before.

John Verrall was standing in the hall. She paused to look down at him, and he in turn looked up. By his appearance he had travelled some way. He had the weary, slightly dusty look that men take from a horse that has tired on the journey. Perhaps for the first time she saw him as he was – a man five or six years her senior, open-faced, short-haired but not cropped; a man of deep conviction, openness, honesty. A man of kindness, of sensitivity. As he looked up at her his weariness seemed to lift. He smiled, yet she knew at once that he had not come for that alone. For the merest second she paused on the stair, merely to savour the newness, the strangeness and excitement of a beginning she should have seen before her long ago . . .

Then she ran down the rest of the stairs crying 'What's amiss?'

'Where's your brother?' he asked. 'I've brought him dismal news.'

Nicholas was crossing the hall as he spoke.

64

'Well?' He frowned and paused and struck his fist on the table. 'I can guess at it! The load's astray?'

At dawn the first cartload of supplies had trundled quietly out of Plashets, bound for Arundel.

'Waylaid and taken,' John Verrall said. 'The drivers beaten and one left dead.'

6

Incident at Staglye

Nicholas groaned and cried out, 'One killed? Who?'
'Morphew – Amos, was it?'

'Samuel's son. A very good, sound young man. A great fine smith already.'

Nicholas sounded as if he might weep. The first casualty of the war to come close – close enough to make reality of a matter that had too often in the past seemed fantasy.

'You did say your men were loyal?'

'Yes.'

'You are very sure . . .'

'I am entirely certain, John. They spoke first. Then I spoke what I should've done a year gone. Then we were at one, respecting each other – brotherly, you might say. My sister know as I know how we held our peace here – how we hung back. Cowardly, if you like to call it so – yours was the stronger part. Maybe its timmersome to pray for a peaceful life and no bloodshed.' Nicholas shook his head furiously. 'No, no! There's no man treacherous at Plashets.'

Verrall did not reply. He looked deeply at Nicholas and then away to Cecilia. He seemed to wait while in the silence between them one thought led to another.

66

'You mean,' said Nicholas, frowning and speaking low, 'you mean there is not only Plashets. You mean there's Mantlemass.'

'Forgive me, then. But I do recall you have a newcomer here.'

'And he's been sick,' cried Cecilia, 'and barely moved abroad. There's been no talk of the matter, neither – there's nothing known of the Plashets work indoors here.'

'It's known I've come and gone, and come again,' John said. 'I spoke of my master's purpose – how he called men to his standard. Any might think what follow. Now, do you forgive what I have to say – but your cousin did speak up powerful hot against the Parliament.'

'I'd go surety for Edmund,' Cecilia said. 'Nicholas?'

He hesitated a second. 'Aye – I trust him. He has a new life here. No other place to go. For that alone he'd not betray us. We are his people.'

'Then we have no answer,' John Verrall said.

'And no redress, neither.'

'His lordship's Mr Stapley has been mighty ardent in these parts. They're working the longest founday I ever saw over to Newbridge. Well, his lordship have claims there, true enough. There's a plenty stout men thereabouts'd think little of waylaying a load and setting it on a different road.'

Nicholas burst out – 'There's brothers and cousins of Plashets men working Newbridge hammer!'

'You go too meek in this warring world,' Verrall said, gently enough. 'This is the way it wags over wider fields than ours. It's brother against brother and father against son all the length of England.'

'Well, then,' said Nicholas, 'we must but watch and see what's best. And you do as you see fit. Sound my cousin Edmund, come you must.' He sighed and straightened his shoulders angrily. 'Tell Giles fetch my horse, sister. I'm for Plashets now. Rest you easy that way at least, John. It's none so many long miles to Arundel – not if the weather hold firm. There'll still be the Plashets Lily seen thereabouts. Plashets men are sworn to it.'

Cecilia went to find Giles and when she returned John Verrall had gone. Nicholas was pulling on his boots. She watched him without speaking, feeling very strange in herself, almost light-headed. Over the years John had come and gone, stopping in whenever his work brought him by Mantlemass, or when he came to Staglye to visit his old aunt, Goody Parfit. Although from his last visit to this she had not greatly missed him, from this to the next stretched to eternity.

'What do you think?' Nicholas asked her. 'Who'd betray us? I'm much concerned. None's been here – no strangers. None rid in since that fellow with Arundel news, that's full three weeks gone. There were naun to be learned of then.'

'There's always spies, you know that.'

'But not easy missed by some eye or another. News gets shoved abroad fast in these parts – you know that.'

'Then – why not news of Plashets working for Parliament?' Then she said, 'There was one other come here, these last weeks. Mr Stapley come.'

'Stapley!'

'Said he come about the deer pale. I said you knew a'ready it needed mending, and so it would be done.'

'You never spoke of it . . . Was he here long?'

'An hour. Maybe longer, though, for he fell to talking with Dorian – '

'Dorian!'

'What could she have known?'

'Not then – but if they met after . . . ?'

'Might they so . . . Oh, aye – indeed they might! They might! What if he set her to spy on us here? She's hot for the King . . . '

'Less that, maybe, than that she find life pretty dismal, year by year – a pretty woman once, and not getting younger . . .'

'I'll tear her hair!' cried Cecilia. 'The gifty effet!'

In spite of his worries, Nicholas burst out laughing. 'That's scullery talk – our mother'd say, surelye. Leave her, leave her, poor soul. If ever anything get to be known certain – then tear come you want to.' He sighed and shook his head. 'The men toiled hard and long to get all that old battle stuff burnished and sharp agin . . .'

Cecilia went with him to the door and watched him ride off with Giles. He might not get back before morning, he had said. There would be much to be talked out and decided. She thought he seemed firmer and more purposeful than she had known him until now; and that was good, but the reason troubled her. She did not want him to profit by disaster, even though the profit be a spiritual one, a confirming and steadying of his own nature.

Cecilia did not sleep much that night. Nicholas had not returned. The rest had badgered to know where he was and what kept him so late. Some trouble at Plashets, she said; and left it at that. She had glanced at Dorian curiously; her aunt was mending the hem of her second winter gown. This was surprising enough to appear startling in its significance. Cecilia lay in bed and thought of this, and of Amos Morphew, who had died youngish. The bitter danger of it all made her chill and shiver. Besides this she had worries of her own about Edmund, of how she had contrived to show proof enough of their relationship, but held back what was most important. She was keeping him from his true inheritance by her wicked silence. She could not do so forever, and when the revelation was made she thought it might kill her mother . . .

But most of all that night, to comfort and strengthen her flagging spirits, she thought of John Verrall, how she had looked at him for years without seeing him; of the strangeness of recognizing him for what he was – the one person she needed. She came upon the extraordinary knowledge that she, who had seemed so complete in herself, was now but half a person – and unless she could be joined to the other half she must surely go maimed through all the rest of her days.

She thrust back the bed curtains and saw the white moonlight lying like squares of bleaching linen on the floor. It was very cold. She would have given much for a sister sharing her bed, one she could wake and confide in, as she could never confide in her mother. Susan was a daughter of the manor who had married a little above her, and so would expect her daughter to do the same. Susan would see John Verrall only as a countryman, the servant of his master – a master who had called men to his colours on behalf of the Parliament.

Cecilia pulled a cloak round her and left her room. The whole cold house was bright from the moon, and she did not trouble to take down the little lantern that hung on the wall outside her door. She went down the stairs, making no sound about it, for the entire structure was of solid oak, renewed in the last generation and carved by craftsmen into garlands and ribands on its rails and heavy posts. Cecilia came to the parlour. There were curtains at these windows, muffling the cold. Rather than make any sound by throwing them clear to let in the moonlight, she lit a candle and set it on the writing table.

'Grandmother . . .' she said under her breath, strangely longing for her, though she did not even know the colour of her hair. Yet now that she had read so much of her writing, Cecilia found this unknown woman in every corner of Mantlemass, indoors and out. The barrier separating past and present was so thin between them that it seemed for ever on the point of crumbling away. Cecilia felt for the spring that held the secret chamber close, and pulled out the great pile of documents. The key came out with all the rest, dangling on its tarnished thread, neatly labelled, mysterious: *The Smalle Chest*. She thrust it back and turned the pages of Ursula Medley's day-book – in her forties when she died, with five of seven children dead before her – Piers and Cecily, Roger and Lewis and an earlier Edmund. All these were family names, repeated over generations. Cecilia's own name echoed earlier Cecilies and Cecily Annes, and made her consider, with warmth and a certain shyness, what she might call her own children.

'The first shall be Medley, grandmother,' she said, hardly knowing whether she spoke aloud or deep inside her imagination. 'Your son Thomas did his best with Mallory. But I shall have Medley, son or daughter I'll never care . . .'

Some pages in the book were so frail that she feared to feel them crumble as they were turned. She peered at the difficult writing, faded and misspelt. '*This day my first son, Roger, did quit us, and for the grave . . .*' '*Sunday: A fine sermon preached.*' '*We toke the hives to hether, me and my son Piers, with four sarvants and my good husband, Robin . . .*' Sometimes in the early pages she called him '*My lov Robin*'. But he was also something other, and Cecilia knew about that, and was the only one in all the household. Because of it Ursula had sent the book, now lost by Edmund, from Mantlemass to Ravenshall '*. . . to mend a quarrell and for the sayke of truth*'. But whether it was the same truth that Cecilia had discovered already and fought with her conscience to conceal, or whether the book held a second secret, she could not know. Only she thought that it had most probably been lost not very far away – that it would be found one day – and carried home . . . They would open it and read it . . .

There was the sound of horses coming up the track to the house, hoofs slithering on the steep bank, then muffled crossing the stream, then thudding into a canter over the last hundred yards. Nicholas and Giles were returning from Plashets. Cecilia locked everything away, took up the candle, and met her brother as he came indoors.

'You never sat up for me, my dear? You'll take a chill.'

'Such a white night – I couldn't sleep. Oh Nick – you do look quite jawled-out!'

'So we all shall be, time this jig's over,' he said. 'I sent Giles to his bed.'

'Sit down, do. I'll take your boots. What have you found since I saw you?'

'Plashets raging. Sorrowing. Amos was Sam's last son of all; one way, t'other way all the rest is dead. It was young Dicky they half slew, but he's spry enough b'now. Only he never saw who come at 'em through the trees. So there it mun rest.'

'Come to the kitchen. We'll take a posset, the both on us, and pray to get some sleep.'

Over the drink he spoke of the loss of men that was troubling him – one dead, one hurt, three gone fighting, three sailing from Plymouth for distant Virginia. 'Wi' fighting and fleeing there'll be never a man or lad left whole in England.' Nicholas sighed and rubbed at his unshaven chin. 'One of the men had news of Arundel – come through his wife's brother, so he tell. The town's fallen to Sir William Waller, but there's two hundred King's men mewed up in the castle. A long seige, they're saying.'

'Oh lord, lord,' said Cecilia, 'I'd not choose to be starved out – naun but a drib left twixt me and cold death!'

The moonlight dropping in through the high kitchen window had been overtopping the candlelight, but suddenly the flame glowed warm.

'A cloud come to dout the moon,' Nicholas said. 'Time for a change of weather. I did see it coming, eight or more days ago, but then it come clear. Please God, we'll have it fine long enough to haul out the next loads and set them on their way.'

By morning the clear cold sky had clouded. The wind had changed. The long weeks of hard, helpful frost were over, and rain would come.

The sudden damp struck at the bones. At first light Cecilia found Nicholas shaking her awake, and she shivered as she roused herself.

'Do me an errand, sister. I'm bound for Plashets straightaway. But do you ride to Staglye for me. John Verrall's lodging with his old aunt, these days. Say the men are with me as I claimed they were.' Nicholas stooped and kissed her. 'Do this for me.'

'For myself,' she almost answered; but only nodded and yawned and promised.

During the morning, Cecilia went to the stables and took out old Cherry. There was no one about, for those who worked outside at Mantlemass these days, worked as occasion called them. Young Matthew, who was good with the horses, was just as good at milking. Cecilia saddled up without calling for help, contented to do so in her increasing need to use her hands. Only as she mounted, Matthew came running.

'I stayed coaxing a drop more out o' poor thin Daisy. I beg your pardon, mistress.'

'It's no matter. Daisy never manage wi'out you – but I set myself up easy.'

She laughed at his expression, half shocked, half sorrowing. She kicked up Cherry, who had seen her best days long ago, but was kind and devoted, and moved out over familiar ground. The clouds that had been big and rolling in the changed sky, had joined and spread and were smoothing out into a flat grey as the wind dropped. What had been colour left from autumn, so sharp and bright in the frost – the beaten-down bracken, the berries, the beechleaves lying sugared with rime in the early mornings – was smudged and lost now, as a few bright threads are lost in a sombre tapestry. Briskness and cleanness had gone from the air. The horse moved over ground softening with every minute, releasing the sharp scent of acorns, but also many less pleasant odours – of mildew, of the last mushy remnants of fungi. The wind had only to drop its feeble sighing and the rain would set in. On the rising ground north and east of Mantlemass, Cecilia paused to watch a small herd of fifteen or twenty deer. They moved slowly, their haunches lean, their bones showing. The frost had been hard and long enough almost to starve them. Some foresters put out hay for the animals, confirmed by custom in a reward for doing so. But hay was short, too, because of the mean summer of that year and the last. The deer would not have moved over open ground in broad daylight unless they had been hard pressed. They did so securely enough today, for they were barely worth the poaching, and certainly not worth the risk of poaching.

Of five villages round about, with fine parish churches with towers or spires, Staglye was the nearest to Mantlemass. It was at Staglye that Mallorys and Medleys had always worshipped. There, too, lay their bones. At one time, Cecilia had learnt from her grandmother, they had intended to build their own chapel at Mantlemass. The building had been abandoned and what remained had long ago been taken for a barn – they still called it the Chapel Barn; its roof was half in and there were not men enough at that time to repair it.

Cecilia rode down the hill into Staglye before noon, crossed the ford and rode on down the street. Goody Parfit, John Verrall's aunt, who had brought him up after his mother died, lived beyond the church, near the mound that was called the Castle. Common sense told Cecilia that John himself was altogether unlikely to be there, but the message she was to leave for him seemed like a talisman, drawing them together, and she was happy.

There were more people about than she would have expected to see. Some newsgatherer was due to ride in, maybe – or perhaps had been and gone, leaving his hearers hanging about to discuss the latest tidings. There would be parents here, anxious to know how things were going, parents of sons who had marched away in the following of one or other of the local gentry. Then she saw that what talk there was was low in tone, anxious and subdued. She called out a greeting here and there and was answered; but none addressed her first, and none followed up the greeting. They stood, two and three together, or little knots of men who seemed to be consulting, little groups of women, pale and anxious. If there was one thing common to all of them, it was that every face was turned towards the church. And by the open gate of the churchyard, she could see Pleasance Goodale standing.

Cecilia dismounted at the block outside the inn, hitched Cherry to the rail and walked on towards Pleasance.

She called out, as she came nearly level – 'Pleasance! What come to this place today?'

Pleasance turned towards her slowly. She was most unnaturally pale, her eyes enormous. She moved towards Cecilia and caught her hands. She was trembling and shaking.

'Pleasance . . . ?'

'A most terrible thing go forward,' began Pleasance. Then she stopped dead, and no more words would come.

A man standing near took up the tale. 'There come a troop o' soldiers, mist'us – three hours or so past. And they did quarter in the church. As being nothing holier than any other roof and walls, they say; nor no worse than an open field, God being in all.'

He paused, looking awkwardly at Pleasance, and clearing his throat.

'Then?' prompted Cecilia.

'Then Parson Lovet thought otherly. And did speak out.'

'So then *they* say,' said Pleasance, breaking in on him, using a strange harsh voice that Cecilia would never have recognized, 'they say they'll hang the parson from the rood loft.'

'Oh dear heaven! They never would do it!'

'They would.'

'Aye, they would do it,' said the man. 'They have him standing two hours gone, with a rope round his neck, and they taunt him cruel – ah, cruel.'

'So then,' Pleasance said through her chattering teeth, 'then my father got sent for. The churchwarden – Walter Chandler – he sent to fetch him, and I come too. I was greatly frit, Cecilia. And so I should be. So Walter Chandler told my father, Get you inside to 'em. They're you're people, he say, and pray alike. So do you go pray 'em now to release the parson. And come they harm him – Walter Chandler say – then harm'll come sore to thee, Advent Goodale.'

This was so strange and violent a thing that Cecilia felt almost faint for a second, even to hear it told. Not least was the knowledge that both these men had enemies, and if either was hurt there'd be some to rejoice – just so was the village divided in these days. She held Pleasance tight by the hand and tried to understand that here in broad daylight, in Staglye, that pleasant place, murder was threatened – tried to understand that this could be even though men as noble-minded as John Verrall's own Sir William had the ordering of just such men as these.

'My father's in there now,' said Pleasance.

Cecilia thought of Chichester, and what had happened there. Her mind slithered between fact and fact – not only the fact of what Waller's men had done, that might have made anyone of sense think kindly of the other side. She thought, too, of the tales that had come through to them of the King's army sacking a village some miles out of London – Brentford, it was, near the river – how they had threatened to slaughter their prisoners unless they changed allegiance and declared for the King . . . There seemed not a pin to put between the two armies.

As if she read Cecilia's thoughts, Pleasance said valiantly 'Soldiers are ever so. My father tell me long ago. Any side, either side – there's naun they'll stick at once it's war. They're that fierce and hot there's not a cruel thing they'd take shame to do . . . It's hate and war makes 'em so.' She moved nearer to Cecilia and hung on to her, 'They're in there. What if neither come out?'

Cecilia put her arms round Pleasance, crying 'Hush! Hush! Never speak it!' But at that instant the church door was flung open so hard it might have burst from its great hinges. Pleasance shoved Cecilia aside and tried to run forward, only the man standing with them grabbed her and pulled her back.

Since the church stood on high ground, when the west door was opened the light shone through from the chancel window. Even on this grey day, standing as she was a little below, Cecilia had a sudden view right into the building. No one had warned her that the church was full of horses as well as men, and she was struck dumb at the sight.

Almost as she grasped what she was seeing, two troopers, bent almost out of their saddles, laughing and shouting, rode out through the door, shoving ahead of them the stumbling figure of a small man in a black gown. It was Mr Lovet. A strange sort of groan went up at the sight of him, as he ran and slipped, and ran again, the troopers holding their horses within inches of his heels. At the gate he fell flat on his face, and the foremost trooper pulled on the bridle so that his horse reared and snorted, its hoofs thrashing above the parson's head.

It was at this instant that a great shout came from inside the church. The troopers wheeled to left and right and turned on their tracks. They left a clear wide vision towards the building and into it.

Pleasance had now struggled away from her neighbour's hold and had run to the fallen man. But Cecilia stood, bolt upright and still, looking into the church, and seeing there something so terrible that it must surely stay with her all her days. She saw the hanging body of Advent Goodale, swinging lifeless from the great beam of the rood loft.

The door slammed and the picture was snatched away.

'Help me! Cecilia!' Pleasance cried.

It saved her from falling, from retching or screaming in horror. She forced herself to turn, to kneel with Pleasance beside Mr Lovet, as almost all the rest standing there surged forward and began to beat and hammer on the closed door, with its great bolts finely wrought, its enormous hinges . . .

'You are safe – safe now,' Pleasance kept saying to the parson.

'Who is it?' he asked, as if unable to open his eyes.

'Pleasance Goodale, sir . . .'

Mr Lovet groaned. He struggled up on to his knees and clasped his hands and beat them against his brow.

'They took him instead! They took him instead! I was their quarry, but he spoke for me. In their sad eyes, that did condemn him. Traitor, they called him; hypocrite, man of the devil, false prophet . . . He was my adversary and then he was my saviour . . . He let them take him in place of me . . .'

7

Year's End

Mr Lovet, the mildest of men, yet had many enemies – it had even been said that he kept his benefice only because his churchwardens chose to support him, lest a newer man took their power from them. Now when they saw him humbled and half out of his mind, many came round, no longer to taunt but to comfort. Their natural neighbourliness overcame their scruples and their opinions. There was a great murmur of voices over and above the girls crouched beside him, but Cecilia, overcome with horror of what she had seen, had eyes only for Pleasance. She waited for her to understand what Mr Lovet had said.

Pleasance stayed a long time sitting back on her heels and staring at the ground. Then she pressed both palms against her forehead, as if there were something inside that must be contained and controlled. She looked at Cecilia at last, turning her head slowly and heavily. Her eyes were clear; they looked enormous, but they were calm.

'They did kill him, then,' she said.

Cecilia did not know how to answer. She felt very sick and simply nodded her head.

'What strange ways we come to,' Pleasance said. She struggled to her feet, smoothing the mud off her skirt where she had knelt on the wet ground. 'I'd best go see.'

Men were still battering on the church door and shouting, and the door opened at last. But then the troopers rode out one by one, shouting as they came to scatter the crowd, striking here and there with reversed pikes, so that cries of pain were added to the tumult. At the gate the soldiers rallied and rode off very orderly and decent, as if nothing had occurred that could ruffle them. Indeed, as they went the last two struck up a psalm, and to confirm or confound the wits of any sane man there, two or three of the crowd joined in and began following them along the road, gathering others as they went.

Immediately, some dozens or so went inside the church. But they did not let Pleasance in until they had taken down her father's body, and laid it decently, closing his starting eyes and doing their best to smooth away some of the anguish from his poor face. They stretched him out on a flat tomb top at the right of the chancel. It was the tomb of Lewis Mallory of Mantlemass and his wife, Cecily, lying quiet there for all of a hundred years. Someone covered the body with a dark cloak, and Pleasance knelt down beside the tomb for a bit, with Cecilia and two or three more. They were all uneasy. There were some there who would sooner pray in a plainer place, and others who would always prefer older ways. There were even one or two who crossed themselves – but so surreptitiously, so muffled by a careful cloak, that none nearby was aware of it. The confusion of thought was great; not only religious thought, but political. There were plenty there who, supporting the Parliament, were appalled by what Parliament's soldiers were prepared to do, and felt their convictions wavering . . . But after a little they rallied and began excusing the troopers. From that it was but a step for the more solid among them to speak out in all the old proverbial ways – how all strife lay at the King's door, improvident and a tyrant, the ruin of his land. And for sure the bad weather, the shocking harvests must be counted against him too, since they were a clear visitation from God in punishment of profligacy . . .

Pleasance had relations in Staglye, her mother's people, a branch of the Ade family that was spread about these parts. Her uncle, Robert Ade, came to find her and said she should go home with him.

'Aye, till they bury him,' Pleasance said. 'Then better I go to my own place.'

'That shall wait,' he said.

'There's none at home milks the goat as she likes . . .'

'Oh, tush, child!' he said, greatly disapproving. 'Come now, come now!' he insisted, drawing her away.

Pleasance knew he had never cared for his sister's marriage and that he liked it still less now. His concern was to get outside the church and hustle Pleasance away to his wife. The girl would have her uses, and could work her keep. A third and final daughter had married and gone from home only last month – his wife was lonely and in need of a companion . . . None of this was spoken, but Pleasance knew the way he thought. Even Cecilia knew a part of it, and she grabbed at Pleasance's hand as she was being swept away.

'I'll come calling tomorrow. I'll send Matthew to milk the goat.'

Pleasance said nothing, but only gave Cecilia a desperate, grateful glance and was past. Cecilia stood watching her walk away at her uncle's side. She was very short and he was a tall man. She looked like a child beside him. He put his arm about her shoulders, but she stepped away. She walked sturdily, her head up. Just once she stumbled and caught at his arm. Then she righted herself and walked again on her own.

When Cecilia had finished telling her tale at home of what had happened that morning at Staglye church, Nicholas said he should go there at once. He looked pale, stern, entirely resolute.

'You're to come with me, sister. Get your cloak. Edmund – go to the stables and see our horses ready.'

'I said I'd go tomorrow,' Cecilia said. She was exhausted by what had happened, and by riding since to the Goodale's place with the news – an old man and his wife worked for them and their tears had not helped Cecilia to check her own. 'Had it not better be tomorrow, Nicholas?'

'What I've to say shall be said straightaway now.'

'For shame!' his mother cried. 'Shall you intrude on her grief? And why should you wish to, for a matter of that?' she added, suddenly struck by the strangeness of it. 'What have you to say to Pleasance Goodale?'

'Madam,' he began stiffly – then softened it. 'Mother – I am to ask her to be my wife.'

For a second there was silence. Susan sat dumb. Dorian, who had opened her mouth to embark on a high-sounding tirade against soldiery, though only Parliamentary soldiery, sank back in her chair deflated. Already at the door, Edmund turned back to smile. But it was Mallory who shamed the rest, bursting into cries of delight that rang out on the stiff silence, running to fling herself at Nicholas, clasping him round the waist, hugging him, stretching up to kiss him.

'Oh – there shall be a wedding feast in this house! Oh, Nicholas, Nicholas – what a fine gimsy delight we shall make of it! Oh, I shall have a new cousin to call by name – and there'll be all the children to dance and dandle!'

'Mallory! Be silent! For shame, Dorian – do you let the girl speak so bold and ugly?' Susan's outraged feelings as usual found an outlet in her sister-in-law.

'Let be,' said Nicholas, smiling and hugging Mallory in turn, seizing her and swinging her round.

'Lord, lord,' said Dorian, languid, 'how soon it be forgot a man died by murderous means.'

'Fair rebuke,' Nicholas said, sobered. He embraced Mallory once more, then went to his mother and took her hands and kissed them very gallantly. 'I should'a said sooner what's bin so long in my mind.'

'You should! You should! I hardly spoke two words to the girl ever in my life.'

'So now we'll all be set to hymn-singing and bible reading and clothes shall be plain and no music heard,' said Dorian. 'But see you, nephew – let her not think herself mistress of Mantlemass. You're but master in name, so let her know that.'

'And let it be known and remembered in this company,' Nicholas replied, 'that since I came to seventeen years old I spent my whole life and strength on Mantlemass and all who dwell in it. And I toiled over Plashets to get us hard funds to keep us. Come I must give all over, then give it over I will and no hard feeling. But till that time come – and I don't see it come yet – then most truly I'm master in this house and my wife shall indeed be mistress.'

He had never spoken so, firm and strong and manly. Although Cecilia was already exhausted, although it must be dark before they reached Staglye, let alone returned, she moved at once to the door.

'I'll come to the stables with you, Edmund. It must be Kitty go to work this time – Cherry done more than her stint today.'

Nicholas caught her arm as she crossed the hall.

'You know I never should set any young wife above your good wisdom, sister.' He frowned. 'I made a scamble o' the telling.'

'You spoke up good as a sarment,' she said. 'I was proud. And I made a choice of Pleasance for my sister long before now.' She laughed, but fondly. 'Still – I'm bound to recall you never asked her yet!'

'Did you never once speak of it together?' he asked, frowning harder now, turning a little pale. 'As girls will?'

'Never.' She was bound to smile at his expression. 'You'll need to be a tender lover to her, surelye. She'll be hard put to it to forget today . . . As I shall,' she added. 'As I shall.'

The rain had now set in and it was in fact a foolish thing to ride out at this time, on however familiar a road. Nicholas groaned at the rain, not for himself or for his sister riding with him, but to think what must come to the ground over which heavy loads were to move from Plashets, bound for Arundel or beyond, however the fight should go . . .

Robert Ade, Pleasance's uncle, had a good solid house fronting the road just short of the village. He had built it ten years or so ago, and had used brick, which seemed outlandish to his neighbours, accustomed to employ local stone for all building. They had thought it a great pretension in him, the place seemed much done over, it was considered. Like the Goodales, the Ades had come up in the world. They had come faster and farther and had many humble relatives in the neighbourhood whom it was easier not to claim.

A servant called Mr Ade to the hall, where Nicholas and Cecilia waited.

'I come to speak comfort to your niece, sir – my friend Pleasance Goodale,' Cecilia said. 'Here's my brother, Nicholas Highwood, rid with me.'

81

'This is a house of mourning,' Robert Ade answered. 'My niece is resting quiet. Another day.'

'Let her know we're come, sir, if you please,' said Nicholas. 'I doubt she'll give us quite such a skinny greeting.'

This was not so civil as seemed wise to Cecilia. She tried to cover her brother's manners by saying how they had brought sympathy from all at Mantlemass. Also they came to ask when Advent Goodale should be buried, that the men of the family might follow the coffin. 'Seeing he was Mantlemass tenantry,' she said.

The word was a mistake, since it spoke of service. Robert Ade bristled slightly.

'I never would've given consent to my sister's marriage,' he said, 'only at that time it was not mine to give – our father being still alive. But if the master of Mantlemass think to have some manorial right over Pleasance Goodale – I have to tell him she shall be a ward in my house.'

When he said *manorial right*, he made it sound as if Nicholas had invoked the old *droit de seigneur*, by which he would be entitled to have his pleasure of any tenant's daughter he might choose.

So that Nicholas answered stiffly, 'I am come here this late afternoon, Master Ade, to ask your niece in marriage.'

There was a silence. Cecilia looked anxiously at Nicholas. In his new firmness he was holding Robert Ade's glance, compelling him to attend and answer. A score of conflicting emotions passed over the older man's face in those two or three seconds – reluctance to be dominated first of all, but last of all a sharp consideration of a goodish match, even though Mantlemass offered less today than it could have done in past generations.

'Her father had nothing,' he said. 'For me, I've provided already for three daughters. There can be no dowry.'

Was it then or some minutes earlier that Pleasance had come silently into the room and stood by the shadowed doorway unnoticed? Cecilia was too intent on the two men, too anxious to be certain.

'I am come for a wife, sir, not a fortune.'

'Her father was a perverse fellow, with his puritan ranting and canting. I doubt what sort of wife she may make.'

'Then how shall she do as a ward for her uncle?'

'Why, sir, my good lady will have the teaching of her. And I think the world never saw three meeker maids than my daughters when they left her.'

Behind them, Pleasance moved suddenly. She came first to Cecilia, catching her hand as she swung round in surprise. But like a bird pausing on a swaying bough before flying on to shelter, she had barely touched Cecilia before going swiftly to Nicholas.

She gave him a brief, sweet smile, then pressed her cheek against his arm and rested there.

'We'll go home now,' she said.

Once begun, the rain did not stop. The hard ways softened and broke. With a team of twelve oxen they hauled out one load from Plashets, none staying them; there had been no further movement or action against them. But they lost the load where a stretch of ground subsided into bog. They lost also one man and two oxen. They had worked like demons, day and night, to get the load made up and defeat at first sent them all plunging into a slough of a different sort, an absolute despondency, a morass of the spirit. Politics and religion may have existed for them, but in a strange distance towards which not one of them turned. Now they were pitched against iron. They pulled the load out piece by piece, working at times waist high in brackish bog. They piled and stacked the stuff, then cut and hauled timber to make a shelter to contain it. It would not be moved further, perhaps for many months. Though no one spoke of this, the disaster might have been avoided if the indolence born of defeat, of the hard times stretching back over many years, had not let the one firm road sink into disrepair. The hard frost, lasting so long, had too easily cheated them into thinking they might fulfil their obligation.

During this time none came, none went, the news and the urgency died in the dark and the torrent of the rain. Was there a town on a hill above a river, and did men battle for it? And all about England did others still march and gather, plotting and arguing, each side villifying the other? Were there colonels, generals, majors who had been only common men till a cause carried them willy nilly into battle? Many brave standards dipped against the sodden earth in those days before Christmas, when the King was at Oxford, his Parliament passing its own bills, his people waiting for victory, one side or the other, and many uncaring which.

At Mantlemass the rain was endured patiently by all save Dorian. Cecilia watched her pacing and sighing and was more than ever convinced that she had some interest abroad. Poor Dorian. She had married at eighteen a man more than twenty years her senior and was widowed long before she was thirty. She was now at that age when a woman sees her life slipping away behind her. If a personable man cast her long glances, who could be surprised if she returned them in good measure?

Rain or no, Jamie at least was for ever out of doors, not forced to it, as others were, but for pleasure. He scrambled about the muddy banks and splashed through water running free and clear down gullies long dry as bone. The fishing pond, not far from the house, was magnificently overflowing, racing over piled stones, shifting them, making fresh channels into the stream that fed it. Many coloured birds moved about the forest, and though Jamie could not name them all he knew them by voice and by flight. Water fowl came to the hammer ponds, pausing to shelter briefly on their long journeys to places none in those parts had ever seen or would ever see. If Jamie Medley had any understanding at all, it was of these matters; but the understanding was too deep and tangled inside his head ever to be ravelled out.

The boy came soaking across the court just short of one dinner time, and Cecilia grabbed him and pulled him indoors.

'Make haste and dry yourself – ask Dolly to let you to the kitchen fire. Else never a bite you find on your platter!'

'Where's my mother to?'

'In the parlour – Nay, Jamie! You'll not set foot on any decent floor till you're clean.' She looked at him and frowned. 'What do you want with your mother?' It was sadly unusual to hear him ask for her.

Jamie looked disturbed, and began as always to struggle and tug away.

'Let be! Let be!' he cried, very shrill. 'Something I have for her – to change for a comfit!'

'What thing is that?' she demanded, her voice sharpening. Was Dorian using him as a messenger – to carry word between her and Henry Stapley? It was not a comfortable thought. In any case, she was not to learn, for Jamie had shut his mouth hard, and once that happened she knew how fruitless it was to question him about anything at all. 'So you'll tell me naun, wicked Jamie?'

'Nay, I willn't! I willn't! I'll tell only Ma'am.'

She let him go and he ran off across the hall. Almost immediately she heard him speak to someone in the closet beyond, that had been a part of the buttery when the hall was used for dining.

'Jamie! You mother's looking for you. Did you get what she asked?'

It was Edmund's voice. For a second Cecilia smelt treachery and sickened at it. How dared Edmund league with Dorian! Then she calmed herself, for he had said nothing to suggest any plotting, merely hurried the boy along. Yet he and Dorian were often together, and shared openly their sympathy with the King. Cecilia would not believe that Edmund could choose to harm Nicholas, but what he might do unwittingly was another matter. One love-sick woman, one headstrong boy – one man of his world to use them, perhaps, as his instrument . . . It was not a happy conjugation. Nicholas should know of her doubts but she hesitated to add to his worries. He had a great weight on his mind already, with Plashets and the doings there.

Nor did she want to take away from the happiness he found at home in planning for his marriage with Pleasance – his delight in finding her waiting to welcome him at the end of each day's labour – solemn, still, from her father's death and the manner of it; but each day more resigned, therefore more cheerful. Cecilia willingly accepted the fact that her old place in Nicholas's life now belonged to Pleasance. If she felt the occasional prick of jealousy, she scolded herself for it. Hers was the lot of any loving sister; she would accept it cheerfully for her brother's sake.

Three days before Christmas, a messenger stood in the hall with news of the world, most of all of Arundel. The rain had eased and the weather grown colder. The change brought fog to shut off half the world. In the silence it laid upon the forest each drip of water along the branches was magnified; coneys bolting among dead leaves from covert to covert seemed to trample loud as passing deer.

'A thin Christmas, masters, for them mewed up in the great castle,' the news carrier said. For they had all gathered to hear him – the family and servants, the workers from the farm. The war, that had seemed curiously withdrawn, swung back across their lives like a great curtain. The messenger was a stranger to Mantlemass and to the forest area, and spoke with a different turn of phrase. 'They'll be skeleton-thin by now, that's my guess,' he said. He laughed, but carefully, a discreet eye on the assembly. He was aware that he had moved eastward – so how did the wind blow in this household, where the masters had been long established but the servants spoke very free?

'Sir William Waller increases his force every day,' he told them, 'with deserters from the Royalists that's under siege – there's man after man sneaks out from the castle garrison. Still – there's Lord Hopton, and his army's said to number many thousand, marching to raise the siege and rescue the King's cavaliers. They say he'll be quartered by Petersfield any day.'

'Did you see any lad of ours?' asked Sarah Akehurst.

'There's two more run off that way this past week,' Giles said.

'One my nephew, Tom,' put in Dolly. 'And I dunnamany more come there from hereabouts.'

'Like my sweetheart Ralph,' said Phyllis from the dairy, simpering, tossing her head because Susan Highwood tutted and shook her finger.

'Well, I could hardly know to'other from which, goody,' the man said. 'There's lads in Arundel from every village I pass through, from there to here. My fellows told me to speak of two names from these parts, though. One's young Sir William Springett, very highly thought of. And then there's his bailiff or steward or some such person, Master Verrall, is it?'

'John Verrall?' Nicholas cried. 'Is he rid to Arundel?'

'And like to be captain, I'm told.'

'In Sir William's own regiment, no doubt.'

'Aye, sir. With many another fine honest fellow.'

Cecilia spoke for the first time. 'What happen, day by day, at

Arundel?' Her voice sounded strange to her, and so it must have sounded to others. Susan looked sharply round at her, and Nicholas, too; for she sounded as if she might be trying not to weep.

'Why, mistress, Arundel's a poor sort of town to be in these times. The house roofs are blown all inward, and the windows gape from the awful shattering of the guns. It all came about when General Waller took the town.'

'The people! The poor people!' Mallory cried, yet enjoying the horror of it, the excitement of amazing events. 'How do they fare, poor wretches?'

'Why, very poorly indeed. There's many fled out into the countryside and won't come back. For what should they come to? The shops are taken for stabling, there's scant trade to be had. And so it goes with the houses through all the decent streets – straw and horses and dung in all and every of their lower floors. Some days there's sorties and skirmishes, and more good men lost. Ah, ladies – a piteous sight it is, too, for there's many sore wounded that'll not recover themselves in this life – limbs lost, bloody bandages, men blind or deaf of the gunnery. And besides that now there's talk of fever running through the town.'

'You tell a tale to frit all here,' Nicholas said soberly. 'How shall it ever end?'

'Why, sir, in victory,' the messenger replied. 'But I cannot say whose.'

At last, his news being told thrice over, and losing nothing in each telling, the messenger was taken to the kitchen for a bite before getting on his way. Sarah and Dolly and the rest surrounded him still, and still there were questions asked and questions answered, and cries of alarm and sympathy and wretchedness. It was a good day for him. He was new to the job, being a player by trade in easier times, and ideally suited to the skilful presentation of news. For he knew how to test his audience, how to tease them into response, raising and lowering his voice, keeping them held on a string of suspense. Best of all he enjoyed a tale of horror, for he was used to playing strong parts, and when he spoke of the horrors in Arundel he was pleased with his performance.

Cecilia came into the kitchen while he was there eating his bread and cold bacon, and drinking small beer.

'Have they bait you well?' she asked. 'Dolly – spare him bread and meat to take with him. Let him take a crock of honey for himself, Sarah.'

Sarah bridled a bit, unwilling to part with any of her stores, but the man's pleasant, grateful smile encouraged Cecilia.

'Did you speak with Mr Verrall?' she asked, as casual as she was able to be. 'If so – is he well?'

'I had only hearsay of him, mistress. Honest, though – no doubt of that. He's well on the way to being colonel, for certain. Gentlemen are always colonels in this war. Though they do say General Cromwell will make plain soldiers into officers.'

'Well – thanks for your tidings,' she said. She smiled at him briefly and left the kitchen, all too well aware that Sarah was looking after her thoughtfully.

Pleasance came out of the parlour as Cecilia approached the door. She could hear the voices of Susan and Dorian raised inside the room, and the sharpness of Pleasance's exit told its own tale.

'How they do yape and arg!' she cried. 'Forgive me – they are your people and shall be mine. But oh I do wish wi' all my heart they had minds wi' two sides to 'em – and that they'd let them turn about every now and then!'

'They'll bide in their beliefs, whatever come, Pleasance. Only they never could tell you altogether why.' Cecilia was standing by the window in the hall. She sank down on the deep sill and leant her forehead briefly against the cold glass. 'As well we decked out the hall for Christmas before that man come, I'd not find heart for it now. Oh why should this come to us, Pleasance?' she said, very low and sad. 'So many dying and set on to die . . . Why must it be our time, that're glad to be as we are?'

'My father'd say it come high time that men speak out and see justice.'

'Why – surelye! But they will speak wi' swords and guns and pikes!'

Pleasance came close and put her arms round Cecilia. She asked softly 'Is it John Verrall?'

'Aye.'

'I never thought how it went with you till now.'

'And I never knew it – not till last time of all I saw him. I knew it then. It came like a new life. But what if I don't see him more?'

'You shall see him!'

'He'll die of some fearful wound,' Cecilia said. 'And never, never shall I know what he think of me. Or if he think at all. The King and the Parliament, both, and all great men in other places – in London and Oxford and such – they took away my love . . .'

Her own words made a quiet echo in her mind. Her grandmother had written: *My grandfather's wife, Isabella, fell victim to those times; and because of how the King acted so she came by her death . . .*

'Well,' Cecilia said quietly, smiling wanly at Pleasance as if she, too, must have heard the words, 'nothing ever changes much, seems me.'

8

A Marriage

On the last day of Christmas, when the green boughs were being taken down and burned, the siege of Arundel came to an end. The news did not reach Mantlemass until a good deal later, and then only the bare bones of it, for the weather was hard again; it had snowed a lot. On the eve of Nicholas Highwood's marriage to Pleasance Goodale, they learnt more, and the messenger was John Verrall.

Cecilia and Pleasance and Mallory had set to with garlands once again, and the hall was decked out as finely as ever in all its long days. They used laurel and bay, spruce boughs, trails of ivy, branches of hazel, the catkins already miraculously shaking into their first gold. Even Dorian, suddenly mellow at the thought of company, was prepared to help, and brought out hangings of red and gold that had long been stuffed away in chests. Cecilia went with her to search them out, hoarded away in a small closet under the big roof. Cecilia had never set foot inside the place before.

'Whoever could've slept here, Dorian? There's still a pallet, look.' She moved carefully among the piled chests and stood looking from the window, filthy with the accumulation of years, and showing her a green sky, it was so old and poor. 'Here's a face!' she cried.

A fragment of glass was propped on the narrow sill. It was broken, but it showed part of a head that might have been that of some saint.

'Hide it or throw it in a corner,' said Dorian. 'That's a Popish thing.' She began tugging at the lid of a chest by the door. 'There's stuffs here we could hang out.' She pushed away a chest that was getting in the way. 'Give a hand. Lord – the dust! We should'a had the servants up.'

Cecilia did not answer, for she was gazing at the box Dorian was pushing out of her way. It was small, iron bound, with a fancy-looking lock. There was no other like it that she could see in that heaped and crowded place. Once more the past nudged up to her shoulder. She chilled. She knew what key would fit this lock. She was looking at her grandmother Ursula's *smalle chest* . . .

Now Dorian was dragging out the heavy hangings, damask and velvet very marked and worn. She thrust a great armful at Cecilia and there was no more time to think of anything but the task in hand. They had to call for help to get all this heavy stuff down the stairs to the hall. It all smelt musty as a cellar, but after a bit the ancient creases began to unlock themselves in the warm below. The girls draped and looped them, catching up the worst places with twists and knots of leaves.

'It's all but paradise!' cried Pleasance.

A buzz of excitement was running through all the house, Sarah and her helpers worked hot-faced and ceaseless in the kitchen. Better times would have made a better feast, but all that could be done was being done, and it was certain no guest would leave hungry. What might happen from the end of the feast until a new season brought fresh provender, the household at Mantlemass did not for this once too deeply consider. The marriage in any case could hardly be delayed longer; there was some scandal already that Pleasance lived single under the same roof as Nicholas. Besides, it was only a week to Lent. Cecilia and Mallory would attend the bride, Edmund was to be groomsman. Jamie had wanted some place of honour, too, and been denied it, and hurled himself almost into a fit in his disappointment.

'Why should he not?' cried Dorian. She brought out her parrot-cry – 'It's all but a surety he'll be master here one day.' She held out her arms to him, an unusual gesture. 'Come to your mother, monkey, and she shall comfort you.'

He ran to her at once, threw himself into her arms – and bit her cheek. The blood ran, she shrieked and thrust him away so hard he fell flat on the ground. Confusion reigned.

'She should not have called him monkey,' Susan said, when she heard the tale. She had been sickly since Christmas, mildly, unaccountably ill, with some pain that Sarah dosed and helped but could not send away. There was a physician said to be skilled in wasting diseases, who lived and worked in Lewes; Nicholas had sent a servant and horses to fetch him to Susan, but he had said the times were too troubled for him to ride so far. Susan insisted that she would be up and about in time for the wedding. There was something about her thin pinched face and great bright eyes that told its own tale, however. She lay and dwindled. On the eve of the wedding, for the first time, she admitted she was too weak to leave her room.

'Maybe you'll get sudden strong and set-up,' said Cecilia.

Susan smiled faintly. Even her complaints had gone out of her. Sometimes her eyes filled with tears, but they never fell; indeed if they had she might have been too weak to wipe them away. Edmund sat with her long hours at a time. He did not say that he was remembering his own mother, but they all of them knew that this was so, they all knew that Susan must die. And looking from her to Edmund, Cecilia was aware of another truth – when Susan went there would be one less excuse for her wicked silence over Edmund's true place under this roof . . .

'How came it that your father sent you to Mantlemass?' Susan would ask Edmund time and again, dwelling now much in the past. 'Had you no other kin?'

'None known, madam. My father had three sisters, married and gone and never heard from.'

'No brother?' she asked, her voice light and distant.

'One that died young – that fell from his horse and was killed.'

'So here is your place,' Susan said. She reached out and touched his hand. 'I did once wish you away from here, things being so hard as they were. Forgive me.'

Cecilia, playing on her mother's mood, took turn about with Edmund to speak of Medleys, of Mallorys long gone.

'Tell of my grandmother,' she would say. And Susan spoke of her childhood, but spoke only of herself. Yet out of what she told Cecilia there came a bright clear picture of Ursula Medley, her humour touched with steel, her warm affections tucked out of sight, yet steadfast in all disaster. It was a strange and certain fact that Cecilia loved her grandmother far more than Susan had ever been able to love her mother . . .

Someone was calling Cecilia as she stood by her mother's bed, rain beating on the window. It was Pleasance who came up the stairs as fast as some wild boy. She was tousled too, from all the hard work of wedding preparation, red cheeked and bright eyed; a long way from the sober matron she was set to become.

'John Verrall, Cecilia! He's here! He ask for you!'

Cecilia went down the stairs as swiftly as Pleasance had come up them, but with more grace, for she felt as if she were flying. The speed of the movement swept and bounced her hair back from her brow and she remembered that she had no cap on and must look far less composed than she might have liked. She saw John before he saw her, as she had done that day when she first recognised what he must mean to her. He had sunk down on the settle in the hall, his head was back, fatigue had overwhelmed him; he was asleep, dropped off with the despatch of a man who has been obliged to learn fast how to campaign. His clothes were dusty, his boots covered with mud. He had lost his healthy, weather-accustomed look; his face was grey, there was such a darkness about his eyes that they looked bruised.

She did not know what to do. She came down the last few steps and stood gazing at him, uncertain, thinking how if this were Nicholas and she were Pleasance she might run and clasp him in her arms and comfort him. She waited for him to stir – half wondering if he would ever wake again. But he opened his eyes almost immediately, and stayed looking up at her unmoving. Then he roused himself. He moved his head as if it had become too heavy for his shoulders.

'Stay quiet,' she said.

He did struggle to get to his feet, but was obliged, grimacing, to obey her. Nicholas came in just then.

'John! What come to you?'

'He's wore right out,' Cecilia said. 'Pour some wine, Nick.'

'When did he ride in? I should've been told sooner.' Nicholas put his hand on John's shoulder. 'How're things, then? You rid far and fast, surelye.'

'Better for being here,' Verrall answered. He smiled slightly. 'But I'll have that wine. Giles took my man off to the kitchen – but here I've waited for succour all this long weary while!'

'Drink, then,' Nicholas said, handing it to him, so hastily poured that it brimmed over. 'Where're you from?'

'From the war. I wish I might say I come fast to dance at your wedding, friend.'

'I never saw a less sprackish dancer! Are you sick?'

'Battle-sick,' John answered. He roused himself and drank and some slight colour returned to his face. 'Forgive me. It's true I came fast and far, not all my news good news.'

'From Arundel? We learnt the siege was over.'

'Oh, aye – they raised the siege on Twelfth Night. We beat off Hopton's forces come to their aid – a fairish turnout of men and horses. At North Marden, that was.' He paused and wiped his hands over his face. Then he held out his left hand, the back towards them. 'Look there! My honourable wound! A full three inches, so that prove I'm a blooded warrior. But I'm no true fighter. War's a foul matter. I never felt a sword go home before. Flesh is easy, maybe – but bone grates, blood fountains. It's all a poor service to a man's fellow men, I can tell you.' He was talking half to himself and his eyes kept closing, his speech slurring. 'They were still in good heart when they came from the castle,' he said. 'But in poor body, poor body. No great triumph, and we knew it. So then – General Waller moving on, Colonel Morley and Sir William, my master, were left to administer the place. Poor battered Arundel.'

'Poor battered John, I'd say.'

'So it is all over,' Cecilia said hopefully. 'And you are home.'

'I stopped to borrow a horse – my fellow's near lame. And to wish joy to this house tomorrow. I heard the news from Henty when I stopped at the forge.'

'Then – shall you not dance at the wedding after all?'

'Sadder matters, mistress. I must ride on. I have not told you my master took the fever and has died. I am carrying this dismal news to the Springetts at Ringmer. We must speak of his burial – how best to bring him home. Twenty-three years old. He made a hard fight of it. His lady got sent for and came, snow and flood, from London. And very near her time, poor soul – so we must pray there's no damage.' He put his hands over his eyes again and this time held them there. 'She gave him great comfort . . . I am so weary I need only speak of it to weep! It was pitiful to see them so loving together.'

'Rest before you ride on,' Cecilia urged him, near tears herself, though perhaps less for Sir William Springett and his lady than for John's distress. 'Stay till tomorrow.'

'No.' He braced himself and stood up, flexing his stiff shoulders. 'I'm a poor sort of mawkin to come wishing joy to the groom!'

At the door he paused and spoke of arms and what should come soon from Plashets – the iron must be carried somehow, and once the material was in hand they had smiths now in increasing numbers as the forces grew better ordered, more self-supporting.

'It's founders we need,' he said. 'There's a long slog to come yet.' He paused a second, looking at Cecilia; then took her hand and kissed it. 'I pray next time be not so long,' he said.

It was too little. Yet it was more than he had ever offered her before.

At the wedding feast Edmund drank too much wine. His face flushed, his hair tousled, he danced wildly with everyone from the bride to Phyllis from the dairy. She was whirling alone in the passageway off the hall, waiting until the invited guests had been plied with the best of the food and wine – for then servants and workers both indoor and out would be let in to join the revelry. It was a long honoured tradition in this house, begun no one knew when, but it must have been many years past. Of them all, only Dorian ever complained, and that she did regularly at Christmas, at New Year, at Harvest Home and All Hallows – the last was falling out of favour with the newer thought. Today she was too much occupied with a guest of her own. She had invited Henry Stapley entirely on her own account. Since nothing had ever been proved against him, and since Dorian was by way of being hostess in Susan's absence, there seemed no courteous way of refusing him entry . . .

'Now kiss me for my pains!' cried Edmund, whirling silly Phyllis round, losing his balance and landing them both on the floor.

Phyllis shrieked. 'My sweetheart'll bannick you sore, master or no – you silly, lippy lad!'

'You may slap him about the face, Phyllis,' said Mallory's voice above them. She seized Edmund by the back of his collar and tugged. 'And I'll get to throttle him for good measure!'

'Ahhhh-h!' gasped Edmund.

'Stand up, cousin. Get you to the pump and souse some sense back into your poor addled brain.'

Phyllis ran off, tossing her head, tweaking at her skirts, and Mallory propped Edmund against the wall and waited for some sense to come back to him. Behind them in the hall the music sounded sweet and lilting, feet stamped and slid and the laughter was increasing as the time went over.

'As well Pleasance's poor father got safe buried,' said Mallory. And added piously, 'May I be forgiven for thinking it.'

There was a great noise of greeting and clapping. The Plashets men had come up the hill with their wives to join the rest indoors; the people from the farm were crossing the yard. The hall would grow hot and hotter, faces shine, voices rise. The good stiff smell of humanity vigorous in its best clothes, of whatever cut or colour, would cause Dorian to fan herself and wrinkle her nose.

'Come back to the dancing,' Edmund said.

'Not till I sober you – you're fully sattered.'

She dragged him to the pumpyard and shoved his head under the spout while she made the water flow with a terrible and freezing gush.

'Mall! Mall – let be, in pity's name! You're worse'n any rough boy I ever knew!'

She threw him a cloth, laughing grimly at the chill water dripping from his nose and chin, running disgustingly down his neck and below his collar.

'And now I'll take you a good walk in the air, cousin. Your better health these times do make you overly perked up.'

'Perked up! Sattered! Overly!' he mocked. 'You Mantlemass people talk rough as your own hinds. Now I'll tell you – I'm fair nett up wi' cold!'

Mallory let her sternness go at that, but not her determination. They laughed together, caught arm in arm, but she still pulled down a couple of cloaks, bundling him into one and herself into the other. She took him by the hand again and drew him outside. The air was bitter, the dark all but down. They ran down the track and then glanced back to the house, windows streaming light across the dusk, dancers shadowy within, music still faintly heard. There were hours to go yet before the bridal pair would be sung and played to their bed and the door mercifully closed on them at last.

'I'll never get me a husband,' said Mallory.

'Why, yes – yes, Mall – you'll be pretty when you're quite grown.'

'I mean, nidget – I'll never *want* one!'

She ran off ahead of him, and he blundered after her. He had had time by now to learn a little of the forest ways near home, and each time he went a bit further, for he had all his health back weeks ago. He was still searching for what he had lost, poking about in dips and dells and leaf-filled holes for the book entrusted to him by his father . . .

The night was very clear as the last of the daylight, a cold glimmer on the horizon, slid into shadow. Though the moon was dark, stars gave light to the open heathland and pricked out the sky above the bare trees in woods where Edmund must have lost himself without Mallory. Now there came up a glow to the north-west, and again, more distant, to east and west. There was no such light of furnace fires to the south, where Plashets lay deserted; they had worked out a founday at the end of the previous week.

'That's Newbridge,' Mallory said, jerking her head at the strongest glow. 'That's iron for the King they're smelting out there. Should be pleasing to you.'

97

'You think with Nicholas and Cecilia,' he said. 'Why not with your own mother – and with your aunt Susan; and with me?'

'D'you think my mother'd cry loud for the King any more – if Henry Stapley should turn his coat?'

'He never will.'

'I know it,' Mallory answered, soberly enough. 'And I shall tell you this, too, cousin Edmund: I greatly fear him.'

'You should not. He's a plain man under his fine manners. And nothing proven against him, neither, in that matter of Plashets iron.'

'Well – he'll ruin us all,' she said.

'So you read that in the stars?' Edmund mocked.

'Listen!'

She grabbed his arm and brought him to a sharp halt. At first he thought she was merely distracting his attention, escaping from being teased. But she was looking away now, still as a stone, her head a little to one side as she strained to hear. They had come out through the trees as they argued, and now paused on a ledge clear of timber save for stumps that would sprout again to give another crop. The place would be overlaid with primroses in a month or so. Though Edmund did not know it yet, Plashets was below. He caught the gleam of water without realising what it was. The pond lay as starry as if the sky had fallen.

'What is it?' he asked softly. 'Deer?'

'Men.'

'They're all at the wedding, surelye!'

'Our men are. Pull your cloak round you tight. Come close after me. I must see who's there.'

She crouched low and went down the slope so silently that Edmund's following steps seemed to crash out like gunfire, like a hammer on iron. Mallory paused at a clump of birch saplings and stayed there, watching. He heard her catch her breath and exclaim. He thought she said something about Jamie. He waited for her to speak again, caught by her tenseness, his heart beginning to thud unpleasantly. He peered through the slender silvery trees trying to see what Mallory saw. Then he found what he was seeking. First a covered lantern making a pool of light no bigger than itself. Then the dark shapes of men, rhythmically, purposefully working. And with this came the sound of wood under a mallet, of sawing – all quite steady and unhurried.

He breathed out, then, beginning to see a picture taking shape – 'What are they doing?'

'Enclosing. They're throwing a great pale round Plashet pond . . .'

'Are they able?'

'Never! It'll be torn down.'

'But why is it going up?'

'The King gave all ponds and foundries and such to the Earl, you know that – it was before the war come. But Plashets belong to Mantlemass, and Mantlemass is a manor in itself . . . The way he think of it, the whole forest's one manor, and him its lord . . . Edmund – go fast back to Mantlemass. Tell Nicholas. Bridegroom or not – he has to know. I'll stay watching.'

He turned at once without protest, knowing that he had no power whatever next to Mallory's bridling rage at that moment. If she said Go, then go he must; though he wondered uneasily if he might lose himself in the dark. He started to stumble almost at once, and he had only gone a hundred yards before pitching headfirst into a great hollow half full of leaves that broke his fall. He was very sober now. But it seemed to him a long time after leaving Mallory that he saw the lights of Mantlemass shining sweetly out above him, and heard the music still playing for the dance.

Red-faced with wine and dancing, the men of Plashets and Mantlemass streamed from the lighted hall and plunged into the dark forest. They stumbled over the first hundred yards or so, but air and purpose, rage and an ancient unturnable stubbornness, quickly sobered them. Most had come to the house on foot, but those who had ridden, their womenfolk pillion behind them, waited for neither horse nor wife.

Nicholas had responded instantly to Edmund's tale, told breathless and scrambled from the haste he had made. He stopped the music, shouted out to the dancers, gave his orders. The company poured to the door ahead of him, with a great noise of bellowing protest joined to the wails of the women whose enjoyment was so roughly brought to an end. On the threshold, Nicholas himself checked and turned, guiltily recalling that he was newly wed. He looked for some glance of understanding from Pleasance, some smile of forgiveness. But his attention was instantly riveted on the one man who stayed behind.

'Pray tell his Lordship, Mr Stapley, that I am bound to admire his strategy. Or that of his deputy.'

Henry Stapley shrugged and smiled, ingratiatingly enough.

'Why, sir, I do assure you – it came out most clear in maps and deeds that Plashet pond was made on common land. So with all other ponds and foundries hereabouts it belongs in the general award made to the Earl by his Majesty. That piece of ground never was a part of the Mantlemass freehold.'

'Plashets has bin tied to Mantlemass, generations past.'

'Oh aye – the dwelling. The tenantry acre – no more.'

'A fair claim may be made by daylight – no call for stealth. Let the law decide, if need be – I've no fears of dispossession. And from now – I'd sooner see no man of your master's under my roof.'

Giles had Garnet saddled, and Nicholas turned his back on Stapley and left the hall. Behind him, Pleasance flung herself into Cecilia's arms, her shoulders shaking. But she was laughing, not weeping.

'I could'a known I'd not be married simple and easy – like any other worthy maid!'

'Oh Pleasance – poor Pleasance! Looking all so fair and gimsy – and no groom to see that gown laid folded on the chest!'

'Wait till I get it kilted up,' cried Pleasance, seizing the hem and tucking it into the waist. 'And you do the same. I'll not stay behind here, tame as a tabby. Give me your hand quick, sister. We'll soon catch up the rest.'

They ran together over ground known well to both, their footing certain, their direction arrow-straight. They came out above Plashets to find Mallory still gazing down from her vantage point, her face sharp with rage and worry.

'Jamie's down there! How came Jamie there – and talking with Earl's men?'

'Maybe someone sent him,' Cecilia said, bitterly.

'My mother . . .'

'Forgive me, Mall. I spoke very hardly.'

'So'll I – if it turn out true . . . They'll battle – you see that? They'll kill each other!' She looked round, her eyes wide and wild, and seemed to see for the first time that Cecilia was not alone. 'Pleasance Highwood! That's your wedding gown down-trailing and gubbered!'

Pleasance only hugged Mallory and kissed her. 'None called me Highwood yet!' Then her laughter ended and she was firm, tough and resourceful. 'Shall they fire the pale?'

'For sure.'

'Then best we gather up bavins to kindle. And lay 'em ready.'

This time it was Cecilia who laughed, but she fell to gladly. She and Mallory and Pleasance began gathering dry faggots as fast as they could, sometimes needing to wrench them from the grip of the night's frost, and crying out as the cold nipped their fingers. They bundled the wood in the skirts of their best gowns, slipping and slithering with their load, down the bank towards Plashets.

However long the Earl's men had been working, they had done a fair job by now. Close on a quarter of a mile of withy hurdles tied fast to sturdy posts had been set up between Plashets foundry and the pond, cutting off one from the other. The aim, clearly enough, was to work round to the line of an earlier enclosure, already once torn down, and now to be set up again. Plashets men had not paused to argue, even to challenge. They had waited only to get hatchets and axes before setting to on the paling. They had rushed straight and purposeful at the hurdles, hacking and shouting, from long experience working in threesomes to a steady rhythm – one hacking, one carrying, one stacking.

'Fetch a coal, Mallory,' Cecilia ordered. 'Take it from one of the cottage hearths. We can start the burning.'

She and Pleasance continued on their way, and began setting kindling along with the stacked wooden pales and shattered withy. Edmund was stacking and grinned when he saw them; but he had neither time nor breath even to shout a greeting.

'Edmund clean forgot the Earl's a King's man,' Pleasance said slyly.

His Lordship's men had withdrawn at once when they were surprised. They stood in groups, watching and muttering, but seeming uncertain how to act next. This was an awkward affray, a civil war in its own right, with many men of the same name on each side. The Plashets crowd merely pulled down what had been put up, but the others were at a disadvantage. To defend, they must attack, using weapons against their own kin, maiming or killing. They were unwilling. If his Lordship wished to defend his doubtful enclosures, then clearly he must bring in men from outside. These were all foresters, all were owed rights over common ground, and they saw the quarrel as his rather than their own. By the time the first stacks were burning well, little more than fifty yards of the paling remained to pull down, and of those who had set it up a mere two or three remained to watch the destruction; the rest had melted away. They had been far outnumbered, they would explain.

The fires warmed the cold clear night and lit the faces of those gathered round them. The rage had gone out of the business. It had been an easy victory. Setting guards against any further trouble, the rest moved back up the hill to Mantlemass to fetch their wives and daughters home.

Nicholas found Pleasance in the firelight, her face and hands dirty, her wedding dress torn, her eyes shining. He hauled her up on to Garnet ahead of him and rode her home with his cheek against her hair.

'Sarah give me a phial of her distilled roses,' Pleasance said sadly, 'and I did douse me in it for your sake. And now I smell all of smoke and ash!'

'You smell foresty,' he answered. 'Good enough.'

As they came up to the house, a man on horseback rode past them and away without any glance.

'Henry Stapley, husband. You beat him sore. That's one battle lost for him and his noble master.'

'Surelye. But one battle did ever lead on to another, my dear heart. He'll try again.'

Of all the household, Edmund was last indoors. He had been a long time watching the fires burn out at Plashets. At the first alarm he had felt something of the terror he had known when his own home was destroyed. But if the pattern was to be repeated, as so often it repeated itself in his head, this was not the time. There had been little anger in the men, only an almost grinning determination to undo what had been done. The speed and the rhythm with which they set about the task had resolved itself into something like a ritual – it had become almost a dance, and the rest had gone home as they might after carrying in the last sheaf of the harvest.

As Edmund came slowly back to Mantlemass, he came to his home. The strangeness of his being there among them drained out of him, taking with it old beliefs, letting in new. He went in by the back of the house, at the kitchen entry, and the three housedogs sleeping by the door leapt up to growl, then sank back when he spoke. He went into the kitchens, and sought about by lantern light for Sarah's great shears he had often seen her using to cut up old cloth for cleaning. There was a square of darkish looking-glass hung near the window and he set the lantern by it. He took the shears and braced himself. Then solemnly and with his teeth gritted, he hacked away his long cavalier locks.

9

A Return

If there were to be another blow at Plashets, a further conflict, it was not yet. In the weeks after the marriage of Nicholas and Pleasance, all stayed quiet. They were left in peace at the ironmill and got about their own business; which was Parliament's. They were running off very fine material at this time. John Verrall had said that it was the founders, now, who were important, that they must be willing to feed the unwrought iron to army smiths. But to forge some of this fine stuff into weapons became irresistible to such masters of the anvil as Henty and Hendall. They laboured long and lovingly; the Plashets Lily was bound to find its way to many distant fields, changing hands, no doubt, with other spoils of battle. It was impossible for any armourer to know whose breast he laboured to pierce.

The conflict had now shifted – to the west and to the north, where King's men were mustering at York. In the south, men still moved and gathered along the Kent and Sussex borders, raw troops to be formed and disciplined, the makings of a great and powerful force to send against the Cavaliers; strengthened and blessed by the hand of God, its leaders would say. Meanwhile, they were a plague about the countryside, with their requisitioning of horses and provender, their intrusion into the churches in search of stabling. At one parish they used the great oaken door of the church as a target for musket practice, and left it full of holes; in another, zealous against the idolatry of painted saints, they shattered the windows. It was all done piously, John Verrall claimed – but grimacing at it none the less. He paused briefly at Mantlemass after the Springett burial, at Ringmer a few miles away – coming and going so swiftly that only Nicholas had any word with him.

'Stay at least an hour or so, John. You'll be sore missed if you go without a greeting for my wife and sister.'

'I'm bound to move on, friend. I came this way most of all to ask for your mother – I did hear she was grievous sick.'

'I think she may not last till evening,' Nicholas said. 'Pleasance is with her now. My sister's quite jawled-out wi' watching, and got sent to her bed for a spell.'

'Then greet her for me, when she wakes,' said John, already pulling on his gloves. 'I am called northward. There's likely to be much movement about the countryside, these months coming. I have no knowing when I may come again. Perhaps never. In war, men come and go fast.'

He and Nicholas embraced warmly. Nicholas did his best to make light of the parting, but he knew there was a terrible, heavy sadness hanging over John.

'God bless you,' he said. 'I shall pray He send you safe back to us all.' Then he added, a shade awkwardly – 'Could be I'd best not say this – but I shall. I've no doubt but you take first place in my sister's prayers.'

'Then tell her . . . No. Best not. She should seek some other – one not pressed by cruel conscience to be a soldier.'

After that he was gone. The cold twilight of early March received him grudgingly, then bitterly filled up the place where he had been. The great house was very quiet and Nicholas felt its weight on his shoulders, pressing him down. His mind and his spirit were sour with the resentment of any born into troubled times, who longs only to be free for the simplicity of his own thoughts. He grudged the fury of his day, longing to live quiet and content with Pleasance, to rear up their children in the love and care of their birthplace.

He heard a slight movement, and Pleasance came down the stairs.

'How dark you stay here, husband. I'll call Giles to bring lights.'

'How is it?' he asked.

'Why, I think well. Your mother's sleeping – Sarah made her a herb pillow. Soothy, she look, and full content. Near to smiling, almost.'

'I wish she might not wake again,' he said very low. 'Is that blasphemy?'

'No, love. No – it is a good wish. She's naun to fear of God, surelye. She say her prayers and fold her hands. The pain go right out of me, she say. Next thing, she lie sleeping and easy.' She went close to him and took his hands. 'I'll wish it for her, too, my dear.'

'We bin often and often to odds,' he said, shaking his head. 'Yet a mother come hard to lose.'

There was a flurry above them and Cecilia called urgently from the head of the stair, 'Sarah waked me. Come quick, now. Sarah think she's gone.'

Perhaps Susan's death had most effect on Dorian Medley. She was lost without Susan to badger and harry and mock. Since the business at Plashets on the evening of the wedding feast, she had been cut off from Henry Stapley. Increasingly she sent him messages by Jamie, letters to be delivered at his house a good five miles across the forest; it was built at the gate of his Lordship's park, that had been enclosed when the King awarded so many rights to a newcomer. Replies were brief; or there was no reply at all. Stapley was either away when the boy came to the place, or his servant chose not to answer the bell – though it clanged proudly enough. After a while, Jamie rebelled. He wept at being sent, then refused to go, then was so chivvied that he would set out with a letter and destroy it on the way, or drop it into the hiding place where he kept his treasures. 'There wasn't none to home,' he would claim, returning to his mother empty handed. So Dorian, guessing his usefulness was outworn, tried to coerce Mallory to be her messenger.

'Dearest Mall – for your poor mother's sake – pray run this errand. Only see to keep it secret.'

'What secret is there?' Mallory demanded. 'Any know you sigh after him. The servants all know – and take their laugh of it.'

'Be silent!' cried Dorian – and lifted her hand. But Mallory was very light and quick on her feet.

'It's true, mother!' she cried fiercely. 'It does shame us all. Pray be rid of him, for pride's sake.'

'He is a gentleman. I see few.'

'He's a rogue, more like. He keep a gimsy girl in his house, and any know she's n'wife n'servant.'

'Oh be silent!' cried Dorian again, stamping her foot, covering her ears.

'Walter in the stable tell that,' said Mallory soberly. But her mother would not listen. She broke into weeping and wrung her hands together. Poor Dorian, who had been beautiful and was still not old . . .

Since the night they tore down the paling, revelling in it, in the brotherliness of working side by side, Edmund Medley had been drawn back to Plashets – and back, and back again. Though they knew he had good reason to profess for the King, the ritual sacrifice of his long hair had been enough for the iron workers. No further declaration seemed called for, for he felt how they moved towards him and heard the subtle change in their voices. Then, what he had resisted had him spellbound, and willingly: the handling of the raw mine, then the amazing moment when it poured molten from the furnace seemed a miracle. Of all things men worked out of the earth that they had been given – what more mysterious and magical than this? From rough veins, dark, blueish, in pale soft stone, to liquid dangerously hissing and flowing, and so to hardness and harshness all but indestructible, shaped by the smith's crafty handling. Edmund saw the great sows of iron cooled and turned from their moulds, and later watched them re-made into manageable bars. But most of all he looked with wonder upon the delicate things certain smiths spun and twisted and beat so gently yet so firmly. Like the device hanging above the master smith's door, the model for all the rest – the wrought iron lily that had been first made, Ben Akehurst told him, as long as three generations back.

'Grover Godman wrought it, my grandfather tell. And it was

first hung at Strives Minnis, two-three mile over the next bank. That site's worked out long since.'

Edmund had never heard of any Grover Godman, and Ben could not recall, either, just who he had been – but some relation to Medleys, that was sure. Ben smiled a little sideways at Edmund, for he had seen many young men come down from Mantlemass to gape – and then to handle iron.

'Let you tie on my son's leathers,' he said, 'and take a tongs, and hold while I hammer. Once a man o' your blood feel the strike, hammer on iron, he'll have it in him till he die.'

'Another day,' said Edmund, taking fright; though not from any fear of using his hands as a labourer – he had used them roughly enough in the months of wandering from Ravenshall to Mantlemass. *A man of your blood*, Ben had said. And Edmund did feel that blood stirring in him, the blood of generations of ironmasters – for Ravenshall, too, had been founded in iron.

He walked home slowly and thoughtfully. His situation troubled him. He had his health back. By rights he should surely be off to join General Waller, to enlist with Colonel Morley or some other local gentleman. He did not want to go. He frankly dreaded the cut and thrust of battle, but it was not so much that which held him back and confused him. This place, these people were now so closely his that he needed to stay near them. He knew well that there was a threat hanging over Mantlemass, and that it might come as much from within as from without. If he was cowardly, it was in failing to speak to Nicholas about Dorian. Nicholas knew of her yearning after Henry Stapley but he seemed unable to take it seriously – perhaps too much concerned with Pleasance and their new life together to feel harshly towards any of his own household. Mallory, though far from a loving dutiful daughter, might speak to her mother, but she would not speak against her. Cecilia, then . . . But her own mother's death had been somehow more her concern than anyone's, and she was still absorbed and distant. Nor did he in fact much want to trouble her with the knowledge of how Jamie had been used as a pawn between Dorian and Stapley. In that, too, he himself was a little to blame, for he had seen and known and failed to intervene.

The early March weather was deceptively soft. Great drifts of wood anemone were laid down like veils beneath birch and hazel. Snowdrops were past, violets lingered, primroses were showing. Along the banks of every small river cutting and crossing the wide forest land, willow catkins were transmuting from silver to gold. It was a time for pleasure, but Edmund was too uneasy to be content. Behind him at Plashets, the trade that seemed so glamorous was the trade of war; five miles away Henry Stapley's master enlisted for the King whoever offered – Irish, Welsh; foreigners in themselves, though not as foreign as some training with them, mercenaries who followed war for profit from land to land . . .

Edmund walked past the Goodales' old holding on his way, calling over the gate to a couple of children playing by the house door – there were new tenants. A man rode by on a black horse as Edmund paused. He nodded a greeting. 'A fair day in these parts!'

His voice had somehow a double ring – it was not altogether strange, nor was it fully inflected with the tones of this countryside. Much the same might be said of his appearance. Well and suitably dressed, he gave an impression of being more than half a foreigner – but a foreigner not from overseas, merely from some other part of England. His horse roused some envy in Edmund, for the horses at Mantlemass nowadays were useful rather than beautiful, save for Nicholas's Garnet.

Edmund came near home, and found that the stranger was still in sight. He had paused on the bank above the river, and stood under the trees that swept on round and down to the fishing pool below. He was still there when Edmund came near enough to see his face, near enough to see his expression. It startled him greatly. It immediately suggested crisis. The man was gazing across at the house softly, with love. He had pulled his cap off his dark thick hair as if in salute.

In sudden panic, half knowing what was to come, Edmund turned in his tracks and began running back through the birch scrub, until he could approach the house from behind. He knew that Nicholas was at home, for he had stayed indoors to wrestle with accounting matters. It was essential for Edmund to reach him before the stranger came to tug the bronze bell hanging at the main door. He began scrambling and leaping in his haste, and crossing the little river at the one possible place for leaping, he missed his footing and got one leg soaked to the thigh. After that the narrow track was easy, skirting the farm over the humped ground covering the remains of old coney warrens, coming up round the far wall of the Chapel Barn, and so to the kitchen entry. He went indoors fast, shoving at the door and letting it thud behind him so heavily that Dolly, in the pantry scouring the stone shelves, cried out in annoyance.

He ran along the flagged passageway and thrust into the hall. He saw the place suddenly as a picture, frozen in time. The pale spring sunlight was falling gently through an upper window, warming the stone, giving it new life. Cecilia was coming down the stairs. The door into the small parlour was open, and inside sat Dorian, a square of tapestry fallen on to her knee, her head back, her eyes closed . . . There was no more to it than that, but it was as if Edmund knew, staggeringly and clearly, that within seconds something would have happened to wipe out that picture and shatter its frame. He recognized a sensation he had experienced at least once before in his life – the moment had the same heavy significance as that moment at Ravenshall when the troopers rode in to the stable yard . . .

It came almost at once. Alone, without any servant to precede him, the stranger had stretched out his hand to the long leathern thong waiting to set the bell swinging . . .

At that, the picture came to life. Cecilia moved on down the stairs, Dorian, roused, picked up her work angrily.

'Who is it, Edmund?' Cecilia called; and her voice was sharp with the hope that it might be John.

A young lad, Giles's son Humfrey, just beginning work in the household, came smart and quick across the hall and opened the heavy door. He was young and short for the task and seemed almost to stagger as the door swung inward. A more modest visitor would have used the small side door.

This one stepped inside at once, very easy-mannered.

'I'll speak with Mistress Medley,' he told the boy.

'Who'll I say, sir?' Humfrey asked.

'Just say a visitor,' the man answered, and smiled.

The boy crossed towards the parlour, Cecilia reached the bottom stair, Edmund stayed still where he was. The two women spun for a second in false hope. If John had not come – then had he sent a message? But the caller had asked for Dorian . . . And she, leaping up, supposed she must find her lover standing there, with invitations to flight, with promises of marriage, with a whole new world in his hands . . . But it was not Henry Stapley, either, nor any sent by him; though he turned to her smiling and holding out his hands . . .

Cecilia had watched her aunt come flushed and hopeful from the parlour. Now she watched the colour leaving Dorian's face, until it was so completely bloodless, lips and cheeks and all, that the outcome was inevitable. With nothing more than a very faint moan, Dorian slid to the floor.

Edmund cried to young Humfrey, 'Fetch Sarah!' then ran with the others to where Dorian was lying. Cecilia was already pulling her, with the stranger's help, into a sitting position, forcing her head down in an undignified manner that would surely bring the fainting woman round very smartly, if only in outrage. And she did stir almost at once, this time groaning loudly.

'Poor soul, I startled her!' the man cried, taking Dorian's hand and slapping it gently. 'I meant only to surprise her. I was a fool!'

'She does take swimey rather easy,' Cecilia said.

'I should have remembered.'

Like Edmund, Cecilia had almost known what was happening, what must follow. Now his *remembered* told her everything. The heavy knowledge of what had to come made her wish she could escape, even momentarily, as Dorian had done. She shook Dorian, and slapped at her cheeks a good deal more firmly than her hands had been slapped. At that moment Sarah came in with a bottle of vinegar salts. She glanced at the visitor – then threw up her hands. She was smiling widely as she stooped over Dorian, for she knew of nothing more wholesome than a family reunion.

'Wake now!' she cried. 'Madam – your husband's son is here! My dear, the master come home after this many year! It's Master Roger Medley, madam!'

Cecilia had said, swift and sharp, 'I'll fetch my brother!' And she had leapt up and run before any other there could speak or move.

She knew that Nicholas was in the room upstairs where Mantlemass business had been worked over for years. As she went up the stairs, light-headed and sick with anxiety, the words of a letter ran in and out of her memory, crossing and twining and tangling. *Master Piers Medley sate offen in the littel writing room . . . Papers was spred about . . . This room was his room . . . There was the names of alle the horses . . . A gret ring was on his fingre, and when that day I come at last to the truth. . . .*

Cecilia went straight into the room, bearing with her the truth she still hoped might never need to be spoken. She stood behind Nicholas as he sat at the table, and put her arms round him, as if she must steady him against the shock. She spoke to him more lovingly than she had spoken aloud since they were children.

'My dearest, my only brother, my dawlin boy . . . Roger Medley come home to Mantlemass.'

Nicholas put his hand over hers as she clasped him and he was so still she might almost have shocked him to death. He moved a little and said half under his breath, 'I am well served for thinking the place were mine.' He took his sister's hands, and held them for a second over his eyes. Then he put her away and straightened himself and asked, 'What's his manner?'

'I never stop to find out. He looks well – dark, like I remember our uncle Thomas.' And like some others Ursula Medley had described. 'He smile well enough.'

'God give me iron to my bones! It's all of ten year since Roger Medley took and left Mantlemass. Six o' them I stood in his place. Where'll I stand now?' He shrugged. 'Letbehowt'will . . . Where's Pleasance? She best hear before she come head-on agin him.'

But Pleasance was running in search of her husband already, for she had found the knot of them gathered in the hall.

'Is it truly him?' she asked. 'What shall it mean? *Can* it be true? Master Thomas Medley's son? Your mother's own nephew? Your cousin?'

'Aye – all three,' said Nicholas. He kissed her and laughed a little. He ran his hands over his hair and went out of the little room and down the wide stairs to the hall, where now he heard the voices of Dorian and Sarah, of Edmund; of another, just remembered.

As Nicholas came towards him, Roger Medley looked up. He was not so tall as Nicholas had thought – a boy when they last met – but he was darker, his hair very thick and curling. He was strong, broad-shouldered, a shade over-muscled, as if he had laboured above the ordinary for the son of even so modest a country gentleman as his father had been. His expression was open and honest. He moved forward at once, holding out both hands, warmly ready to embrace Nicholas as a brother. Only Nicholas did hold back a shade. He had to give what Roger would take, and his situation was therefore one of caution; he would not fail in his clear duty – but he could not succeed in it with any willingness or pleasure. For all his protestations of stewardship, he had been his own master too long for this to be an easy moment.

'Nicholas!' Roger cried. 'Is it? Yes – Nicholas! I left you a lanky lad. Now here I find you a grown man with a fair wife.'

'You may drop water into an hour glass,' Nicholas answered, 'but that never stop a day from ending.' He grinned, but it was a difficult grimace. 'You spent many a year finding a way back to these parts, cousin.'

'Too many. I have a long tale to tell – but later. I have found a new cousin here – Edmund Medley. We go pacing round one another like cocks at a main! Tell me, Nicholas – am I welcome?'

'How otherly? I've a tale to tell, too. An account, see you – an account of my stewardship . . . We'll drink to your return. Sarah, see to it, my dear good soul.' When he spoke to her so, Nicholas was expressing only his warmth towards this old servant; but the words came out, he was certain, altogether too masterly – he was sure he saw Roger flick his eyebrow. 'And, Sarah – let you and Dolly and the rest set about making us a feast for dinner time. Not every day the Master come home.'

Sarah was smiling and beaming, having already had her cry. She glanced from one to the other, not altogether certain how the mood was going. She had known Roger Medley from the day he was born, she had known and cherished his cousins since early childhood. She was privileged as any such old servant of a family must be. She opened her mouth to speak, perhaps to ease her

113

uncertainty, but she had no chance to say a word; Mallory's voice was raised somewhere beyond the hall, and she came in fast, dragging Jamie with her and scolding fiercely.

'He go headfirst over the pinnold rail into the river!' she cried, shoving him ahead of her when she saw their mother. 'He go maundering along and slip on the mavin – and in he go . . .' She broke off and stared at Roger.

'Who's here?' he asked.

'Mallory,' said Dorian, her head dangerously high and proud, 'give a greeting to your brother.'

'My brother?' cried Mallory scowling. 'Greet *Jamie?*'

'Your half-brother, child – Roger Medley. Who was gone from Mantlemass all but before you were born . . . Your father's son, girl, by his good first wife,' Dorian snapped as Mallory's stupefied expression failed altogether to improve.

'I barely got settled to a new cousin,' Mallory said. 'Cecilia – you got Edmund truly cousined for us. Is he,' she jerked her head rudely, 'is he indeed my brother?'

Cecilia smiled briefly and said she must not doubt it.

'Mallory – do I remember Mallory?' Roger asked, recovering himself at this rough rude interruption, and smiling at her.

'Ay, you do remember,' Dorian said, her voice vibrant with dislike of all he stood for, from his mother whom she had succeeded, whose ghost she had never quite banished, to his own superior standing over every one of them there. She held out her hand to Jamie, soaked and shivering, mud in his hair, hair in his eyes, his mouth hanging open as he tried to worry out what was being said. He moved to her slowly, never taking his eyes off Roger, tripping over his own dirty feet. 'Embrace your long lost brother, Roger Medley,' Dorian said. 'Here is my son James, your father's last born child.' And she pushed him hard across the floor, so that he stumbled and half fell, recovering himself by grabbing at Roger with his wet, muddy hands.

'Easy, easy,' said Roger, as he might to a fractious hound. 'Lord – you brought in a fine stench from the river, brother James. Are you sure you didn't pitch into the midden, rather? Best ask your sister to take and clean you – then we can embrace as brothers should.'

Mallory went reluctantly, for she was bursting with her own particular angry excitement. She tweaked at Jamie and whispered something, and he followed her quietly, though never taking his eyes off Roger as he went.

'He is not always so,' said Nicholas, sorry for Dorian, sorry for Roger, too, who looked so much dismayed. 'Our family's not always without such blemishes – as well you know. Your own brother, Simon . . .'

'Aye – he has a slight infirmity of the speech,' said Roger quickly. 'But he has his wits, I thank God.'

'He is not with you,' Cecilia said, anxious to distract every one of them there from poor Jamie. Her head was whirling still with the suddenness of it all, with the significance of Roger's return, so much greater and stranger than any one of the rest of them there could know. 'Shall he come soon? And are you wed by now? And have you children, cousin? How much you shall have to tell us! We'll sit long over our supper, surelye!'

'And you,' said Roger, firm but in no manner aggressive, 'you shall have much to tell me. Till yesterday when I rode through the town and spoke here and there, I knew nothing of my father's death. I should've been sent for.'

'Where should we send?' Nicholas asked. 'None knew where you and your brother were gone. No word of you in all the years. We did think to set about seeking you – but it's a wide world to find one man in.'

'Truly. And indeed it was better for you, did you not find me.'

Still he spoke gently, and there was no malice in his voice or his expression. But his eyes were very steady, his manner authoritative. Nicholas turned slowly red, and felt Pleasance beside him bristle and lift her chin. He glanced at Cecilia and was alarmed by her expression, she looked so stricken. It was Edmund who broke in on the moment, held between them by so delicate a balance.

'You kept silent, too, sir. You did not send to Mantlemass. My cousins have told me so.'

Roger sighed, then, and shook his head. 'I'd left my home and persuaded my brother to follow. There were many reasons – difficult times – changes . . . My father would find hard to forgive me, I thought.'

'He ever spoke soft of you,' Dorian cried. 'I never saw the sense of that – for you two sons, who should have been his support, left him in those hard times. You must needs go your own ways. I know! I know! It was for your dead mother's sake – you never could abide that he married me!'

'Madam,' Roger said quietly, 'I do take blame for much. But I am come now to see how Mantlemass fares. The war, madam, and what comes from the war . . . I must know how my own home stands.'

'Then – look about you!' she cried.

'I do see it rot a little,' he said, very low, and letting some hint of his forest origins slide into his voice for the first time.

'Since you're back to be master,' Nicholas said flatly, 'I'll set about an account of things. It's all bin honestly done.'

'Do I doubt that? Cousin – you do wrong me a little. You're out o' the world here, surelye.'

'Not out of the war . . .'

'Out of the world that deal in worldly matters. Do you know naun of the covenant that the Parliament imposes on landowners? A King's man of property must abjure allegiance to the Crown, and pay a stiff fine for his treachery, too – or else see his whole estate sequestered – purloined – entirely filched from him. For all our sakes, I must sign to keep Mantlemass for Medleys and no other. But the fine may be heavy – for so they mostly are. You look fair miffed and huffy, cousin Nicholas – but you'll see for sure that I must know how Mantlemass stand. This is hard fact. What else can a man deal in?'

'Well, never fear for fines,' cried Dorian. 'Nicholas Highwood was no more'n a boy when your father died. It was that boy took Mantlemass in hand. Aye – and Plashets, too. But never suppose,' she rushed on, giving with one hand, taking away with the other, 'never suppose that Plashets blasts out iron for his Majesty. No, by heaven! Your steward come to be a good Parliament man. And his sister think likewise, and proud of it. She'd marry a man fighting against the King in the field if he would but ask her – never flounce, my girl; it's plain to see. Even Nicholas's own wife is daughter to a snuffling dissenter. So you see plain how matters stand. A month gone I'd have said only Edmund and I were still loyal – now I say only that I am . . . All the tide runs for Parliament hereabouts, Roger – yet the most powerful man now over the forest had his rights from the King himself, and holds 'em fast. We've a war at home and a war out of doors and a war over all the countryside and cities of England!'

When she had finished, Dorian was all but panting, and she flung herself back in her chair and put her hand to her mouth and the fingers trembled, and her eyes filled with tears. She spoke grandly enough of the war and of the world and of loyalties, but what she saw most in that moment was how her own life had run out of the true, and it was all but too late to mend the matter.

For Cecilia it was as if a wind were rising about them all, a tempest that might sweep them all away. She shivered with the pressure round her heart, against her temples. She clasped her hands tightly, whitely together, and hardly knew which face might offer her some comfort. She glanced at Nicholas, Pleasance moving close and closer to him as if she would support him actually and physically – at passionate, unreliable Dorian – at Roger himself. He was stern, now, but still not harsh. She thought he would never be harsh, nor hard even – only utterly, faultlessly steadfast.

At Edmund Cecilia dared not look. It needed only one more declaration from Roger – then the truth only Cecilia knew must be spoken.

10

The New Master

Roger was silent a long time after Dorian had spoken and a heaviness settled over them all, a mood of blackness near despair, for it seemed as though so much lay ahead it could barely be contemplated.

'How shall I tolerate this?' he said at last. 'It 'maze me utterly – utterly. Any man knows of disaffection in the south and east – but this land has ever been Crown land – a royal chase, forsooth . . . Such change, then. And did you, cousin steward, impose these views of yours on simple Plashets men?'

'Simple? They know what to think and what I should think with them. We come long months ago to understanding of this. They'll not change. You'll recall, maybe, the great stubbornness of men born in these parts.'

'But I am loyal to the throne, Nicholas – and Plashets is a part of Mantlemass – and I'm master of Mantlemass.'

'No,' Cecilia said. 'No, Roger. No – no – no.'

She spoke very loudly and flatly, sounding like a stranger, so that they all turned to her sharp and astonished – for surely she had lost her wits?

'Now pray listen!' she cried. 'You know well how I've learnt so greatly about Medleys – and so I could tell why Edmund come to us here . . . There is something I know, and I kept it fast since I learnt it – and I do know, indeed I do know I should not! But there were many reasons – and one less, since my mother died . . . No!' she insisted, as one or other of them began to speak, to cry out and question – Pleasance even rose up and moved to her as if she must be sick and in need of help, only Cecilia thrust her away. 'You must listen to me. You must all listen. Only let me think a little how best to say – what I am bound to say now.' For she could not think how to begin. There was so much to be told – and argued – and understood. And yet how easily, how painfully easily proven.

'Will you not have me for Master of Mantlemass, then, Cecilia?' Roger asked.

'No.' Because she heard a faint mockery in his voice her own hardened. It sounded firm and harsh in that high-ceilinged place that always carried its own faint echo. 'No, Roger. For you are not master. Nor ever one of us that come of our grandmother's line. Not Nicholas. Not poor silly Jamie, nor your own brother Simon. Not one of us, son nor daughter. It go all the other way.'

She was standing upright by her chair, and now it was Nicholas who came to take her hand, as if to help her.

'Something from our grandmother's letters, then . . . ?'

'Aye, there – with all the rest.' She pushed him off, too; she had to stand alone.

'Other way . . . What other way?' asked Roger, frowning.

'There were three brothers,' she said, shutting her eyes, clasping her hands together, standing there rigidly and repeating something learnt with some anguish and learnt by heart. 'And a quarrel. One brother went his own way – as you did go your own way in a different time, Roger. That was Harry Medley.' This time it was Edmund who cried out and tried to break in, but the rest hushed him. 'That line – Harry Medley's line is the true one. Our grandmother, Ursula, was a Medley through her mother, but it was by no lawful joining. Nor her husband was no true Medley, but only a son by adoption . . . The blood – the Medley blood – come to us through her, Nicholas – but the name got carried falsely, out of law and wedlock.'

'And do you think to prove this?' Roger said, almost laughing.

'It's all writ down! See it – you'll know as I do.'

'Well, then – who shall we call master?'

'Our cousin mean me, Roger Medley,' Edmund said; and as if to prove the affinity he in his turn slipped into the country tones and usage he had so often mocked in the rest. 'My father come of Harry Medley's line. He ordered me to Mantlemass. With his last breath he ordered me. I see why – I see it plain, first-time-ever. There was a secret. He said so as he died. A secret for Mantlemass. Only I lost it – I lost the book that should learn us all the truth!'

'We mun be very steady now, sister,' Nicholas said. 'For all our sakes, there must be no doubting. It must be proven firm and fast, that none ever doubt it. Else, we'll have our own war till the end of all.'

'Best pull up to the table in the parlour,' she said, smiling at him faintly, already weary. 'I'll fetch the papers . . .'

It was all there, as Cecilia had said. After the letters had been read out, then passed among them and when the sketched line of inheritance on its time-darkened paper had been handed from one to the other, for some time no one spoke. Then Dorian, who, when they first moved into the parlour had flung herself defiantly into the chair at the head of the table, rose, and moved away, and went to sit huddled by the hearth. None else stirred, and the silence spun itself web-like over and about them.

'We do see Dorian's meaning, Edmund,' Roger said at last, very quiet now.

Edmund thought of his father, knowing that he had been sent to Mantlemass not merely for succour, but to claim what was his own. He thought of the dead man lying quiet, the tumult outside, the terror he and poor Harry had known. As if acknowledging a debt, he got up from his place and went very slowly to the table's head. He gave a quick glance round at them all, but there was nothing he could see to stay him. He sat down in the big chair, its heavy oak carved and polished. He felt the great weight of time and death tossed into his hands, the weight, too, perhaps, of love and hatred. What did they feel now – Nicholas Highwood and Roger Medley? Of the women, Pleasance sat still by Nicholas and never took her eyes off his face. Dorian by the fireside had covered her eyes with her hands. But Cecilia still sat looking down at the papers spread about the table, and laid her palms flat over them, as if in some way confirming and compounding – less with what they had made clear than with the writer who had striven hard and honestly to set down what must have injured her severely, struggling to write honestly of a wrong left to the future to resolve.

'When Master Piers was on his deathbed,' Ursula Medley had written in her thin careful hand and her wild spelling, corrected and over-corrected, 'he sent for me and kept me close with him while he told this tale: That my mother Lilias was his natural daughter; and so I was his grandchild. I was not, as I had been let suppose, his daughter by marriage, since my husband, Robin, was Medley only by adoption; he had lived since childhood as Master Piers's son, but was in fact son of a boyhood friend of Master Piers, named Halacre. So then, Master Piers said to me, the true line of inheritance go through my oldest brother, Harry, who took his own way many years past, and bides now I know not where; and all I know is, his living has ever been in iron. Only, he said, never doubt you share my blood. In that blood, says he, lieth the strange secret come to us from my father's father, and from his father. This secret he had told my mother, and now told me, and the matter of it was held in an old book, where a certain name was written . . . After Masters Piers had died, I sought out his brother, Harry Medley, by means of lawyers. To mend a quarrel and for the sake of truth, I sent the book to him and never saw it after, nor knew if he came by it, or if it were lost . . .'

It was Edmund who had groaned at that, thinking of how he had stayed at Ravenshall while it burned, and found the book, and cared for it, only to lose it at the last. So that, when so much was made clear, there must remain a secret that could never now be told.

There was still the *smalle chest* that Cecilia had recognized in the little chamber up under the roof, the time she went with Dorian to find hangings to deck out the hall at the time of Nicholas's marriage. There was still the key on its tarnished thread, that she had found hidden with the letters. After supper that night, after they had all sat either silent, or speaking hotly, one over the other in a confused and troubled fashion, Cecilia decided what was best to do. She had always imagined that one day, when by some miracle or magic all other claimants to Mantlemass were lost, she would open the chest for Nicholas. But it was Edmund she took with her after all.

The little room smelt greatly of age, and when Cecilia set down the candle it flared draughtily, and the wax ran ghostly down its side.

'Some one of us spent much time here,' she said. 'But who shall say which? It was a long time ago, surelye.'

She showed Edmund the fragment of glass, with the strange saint's face, that she had set back on the sill after Dorian had bid her throw it out.

'And here's the chest,' she said. 'What if it be the wrong one? Or empty?'

'But my father had just such a one!' cried Edmund. 'It's very twin! What do you suppose? Was it brought to Ravenshall from Mantlemass long ago? When Harry Medley went from home? My father kept the book in it. The book – the book! Lost by my blundering!'

'You were sick. But while you had it – did you never read in it?'

'Once I opened it. It was in Latin. Poems. Then Barnaby stitched it into leather for safety, and so I never looked at it again ... Maybe, even now ... Might it lie still safe and hidden?'

She shook her head. Too much weather had come and gone over the forest by now for anything so frail to stay safe. Even leather saturates, lying long in a damp dank place.

'I think you lost it before ever you got nigh this house,' she said. 'Else one of us must have stumbled on it – even if it were only Jamie's dog. You best forget it, as all us must. What's a secret, if it be found out?'

She tugged out the little chest, that was no bigger than a Bible, and crouched down to fit the key to the prettily ornamented lock. Her fingers shook, and the key would not turn at first. Edmund put his hand over hers to steady it, and there was a rusty grinding, and the key turned a little. Then they coaxed it, and it turned double, and then there was only the matter of being bold enough to lift the lid.

First there were more sheets of paper, but not letters this time, and in an older hand than Ursula's. They were long lists and strange tables – they were the names and pedigrees of many horses that had been bred by Medleys years ago, at Ghylls Hatch. They read like a fine litany. Then came a copy of the attempted family pedigree that was among the horde of letters in the writing table drawer. There was also a sheet of old parchment, very frail at the folds, and on it was drawn to scale the design of the iron lily that was the mark of Plashets work. Next, very much moth-eaten, they took out a roll of tapestry, a piece cut from some much larger work, by the look of it. It showed a bird flying with a branch in its mouth.

'I know of that! cried Edmund. 'It is called *the lark and the laurel* – it is a crest come from the Mallorys. My father had a ring with that design – come down from his grandfather, so he said. But the story went it was only a copy of the true seal – that was lost or elsewhere.' Edmund shook his head, remembering. 'My father wore it always. I almost took it from his hand . . . But it went with him when Ravenshall burned.'

Cecilia had pulled out something more, wrapped up in a kerchief.

'Edmund! It's here! What you called the true seal! *The lark and the laurel!*'

Pinned to the kerchief was a small paper, very hard to read, but in Ursula's now familiar hand. Holding the candle dangerously close, almost scorching and losing it, they made out the words: *Worn ever by Master Piers Medley. Set here for safekeeping.* And then, below, in smaller writing still: *My mother had it once.*

Cecilia looked a long time at the big ring lying on her palm. Then she held it out to Edmund. 'It go wi' Mantlemass. So do you take and wear it.'

'Since Mantlemass come to me,' he said doubtfully, 'shall Nicholas have at least the ring?'

'I tell you, they go together. Take one, take both.' Her voice had sharpened. For what sense or purpose could there be in making any but a clean cut of it? Nicholas had cherished Mantle-mass all these years – but he would scorn to be rewarded.

'There'll be no single head to this house, cousin,' Edmund said anxiously. 'God knows I did feel a King on his throne when I took the head of the table. But I must never feel so. There must be a parliament at Mantlemass!'

'Aye – but wear it,' she ordered, though this time she smiled at him.

So Edmund slid the ring onto his finger, as if he wedded Mantle-mass by the action. He felt a curious shyness in doing so – he might almost have wept.

'That's all the box hold for us,' Cecilia said. 'And it is enough!' She sighed and sat back on her heels. 'Do you hate me, cousin, for keeping silent so long? I did truly think it could kill my poor mother. But most I could not bear it for Nicholas.'

She dusted out the box with the kerchief that had held the ring, turning out a powdering of dust where worms had burrowed, and many paper-dead moths and creeping things.

'One thing more,' she said.

She held out a steel pin, rusted, with a few small feathers attached. As she brought them into the air they stirred for less than a second and then fell into such tiny particles that they disappeared. Nothing was left but the brittle spine of one feather larger than the rest.

'Some ornament,' she said.

They put everything back and carried the *smalle chest* downstairs.

For Dorian, who had ever set herself rather high – and kept her opinion of herself while she grew slovenly and complaining – the tale left to them all by Ursula Medley was the bitterest blow of her life. Her father had been in a small way, though a gentleman of sorts, and her marriage to widower Thomas Medley had been a good match for her. But now she found her children denied their rights and her dignity quite destroyed by the knowledge of her legal situation. She went through and through Ursula's papers, disputing and snatching at straws, saying that she would have lawyers seek into this claim before she would believe it. *There*

were three brothers . . . and one brother went his own way . . . Dorian
was ready to denounce Edmund as an impostor, only what he
could tell her exactly tallied with what Ursula Medley had
related.

All this took away from Dorian her last vestiges of pride. She
must escape at whatever cost. And though she should have known
by now that Henry Stapley, though he had dallied and flattered,
had done so idly – yet she saw him as her only hope for the future.
In her wretchedness, she went to seek him out herself; for she had
now, she felt, nothing in life to lose in the way of dignity.

There was a strong southerly gale blowing as Dorian rode
across the forest to Stapley's house. She had spent time on her
appearance. Her dark dress was well brushed and she wore a hat
with a blue feather. The feather had been Susan's, that Dorian
had raked out stealthily from among the dead woman's unsorted
belongings. In spite of the emotional upsets of the days since the
truth had come out, she still looked much younger than her years.
As she rode, she chewed her lips to redden them, and every now
and again fiercely pinched some colour into her cheeks. The noise
of the wind tossing and battering the trees, where green was now
showing, increased Dorian's nervousness of what she was about.
There was such a roaring she might have been walking beside some
great sea that came curling and breaking to overwhelm and sweep
her away.

She was saved the necessity of going as far as the house. A mile
short of the deer pale protecting the Earl's land, she met Henry
Stapley riding alone. To her enormous relief, he seemed pleased
to see her.

'Now look what this rough day has blown me!' he cried. 'Do
you ride my way? Shall I tell you that you have been much in my
thoughts, mistress?'

'Tell me any truth,' she answered lightly. 'And which way is
your way? I came from the house to be alone.'

'You should never be alone,' he assured her. He was a good-
looking man, easy on horseback. He smiled and eyed her in a
manner that made her lift her chin and return his glances with all
the provocation she could muster. The little blue feather curled
against her cheek, her dark hair was soft under the hat's brim. 'And

you are too bold to ride unattended,' he assured her, 'a woman of your beauty and your youth.'

'Then indeed I had best ride your way!' Dorian cried. 'And you shall be my protector!'

They turned side by side into a long ride between birch trees lively with the wind. Stapley continued to make gallant conversation, dealing in local small talk but somehow contriving that every word of it should ring with significance, and Dorian responded readily, with laughter and with such replies as she hoped might make him laugh in his turn. And he did laugh, for though he was a bit of a rogue, as well she knew, he was still gentleman enough to give her the attention she so much desired.

'I count myself on holiday,' he said. 'I did not know it till we met. Now I see the day is mine. Or shall it be ours?'

'Let it be ours,' said Dorian.

She kicked her horse into a canter, and Stapley came after her, and the pattern of flight and pursuit was thus readily established. The day became bright for her; it shone and sparkled with promise and the bluster of the wind was forgotten. She would escape from Mantlemass, as in the dark nights she had known she must. She took her horse on, through beechwoods now, to that high upland stretch of open heath that had suddenly seemed to offer her a destination. And soon she was leading him among ruined buildings – the walls and broken arches of what had once been, so it was said, a king's hunting lodge. No roofs remained, but it was plain to see at least the shape of the chapel that had served the place. The line of nave and chancel was still drawn a foot high, while at the west end half an archway, with mouldings and corbels, stood as it had done for years, awaiting final collapse. Dorian dismounted and went within the remnants of the chapel. Still leading her horse, she went to sit on the mound of stone that must once have supported the altar. It was sheltered there, the pale sunshine quite warm.

Stapley followed Dorian and took her horse, tethering both to one of many elders grown up shabbily against the ruins. Then he came to sit beside her.

'We are not met once since your cousin's marriage,' he said. He glanced at her, but she was gazing at her hands. 'I thought best to keep away. I was blamed, I know, for the matter of the enclosure that night. The attempted enclosure,' he corrected himself.

'And were you not?'

'I work in the interests of my master. But it was your son Jamie – excellent if excitable messenger – who ran as he was told to give the word.'

Dorian laughed outright. 'He went because you sent him . . . And I sent him, too – often and often – to your house.'

'It was best, just then, that you and I should not seem acquainted.'

'And now – ?'

He did not answer that, but asked a question in his turn. 'Is it true there's a strange face at Mantlemass?'

'Not strange. My husband's eldest son.'

'Well?' he said, as if prompting her. 'And what shall that mean to you?'

Dorian began to tremble. She twisted her hands together and her eyes filled with tears.

'That I am driven from Mantlemass,' she answered, and there was no artifice at least in the way her voice shook and died. 'Aye, I must go,' she rushed on, 'for I have no place there now. So long – so many years, and no sign or sound from either son . . . Now – this!'

'So there is a new master, then.'

'Indeed – a new master,' she agreed; but saw no need to let him think other than that Roger Medley was the one.

'Shall that mean other changes? Plashets? Does your stepson profess for the King? Shall they smelt out Royalist iron now at Plashets?'

'The new master,' said Dorian carefully, 'is for the Parliament. I have heard him say so.'

'Then curse him for that, too!' he cried, suddenly violent. 'His Lordship shall not tolerate it long. Come sooner, come later, he'll take what's his. And maybe not only Plashets, neither, for the one stands with the other . . . Aye, indeed, I think you should leave Mantlemass.'

At this Dorian broke into tears, crying where should she go? And that she would not stay to see her children slighted.

'He will not fail to care for them, I should suppose,' Stapley said, rather cautiously. 'His own father's children?'

'His own father's . . . ? Oh indeed, yes!' she said hastily, perpetuating the lie by letting Roger seem the one responsible for all her woes. 'Indeed – they will always be cared for. They will be well enough, whatever come to me.'

'Well, then, since that is certain – and they will be safe and secure – and best with their own kin, no doubt – where shall you go without them?'

'Help me!'

He put his arm round her and drew her against his shoulder. 'But shall you help me?' he asked softly.

They sat there a long while. The sun shifted and they were in shadow, and Dorian began to shiver. But she dared not move, or break in upon what he was saying, for the whole balance of her life was changing. At first she was aghast that he should be so frank in discussing what was afoot. But then she came to see that if she betrayed him she must betray herself – and she never would, for vanity, as he could easily recognize. She would never speak of what Henry Stapley told her that afternoon and lose what she might gain if all went well.

'And after,' he said at last, 'I am called to the north. I am no soldier, nor asked to be one. But I am his Lordship's man of business and shall see to his interests there.'

'So far – ' Dorian said, troubled.

'Well, well – I do not need to go alone!'

She smiled and clung to him, and could not bring herself to speak of the *gimsy girl* he was said to keep at home. Only, if such indeed existed, Dorian knew she was pledging herself to take that place.

When all was done, he was saying, there would be a servant waiting with a horse, and she should join him then. But he would not or could not say when this would be. Nor was she to send to him at any time, but he would send to her in due course. And let her have no fear but only patience and steadfastness.

The demands were great, but for Dorian the reward seemed sufficient. She rode home, chilled to the bone. Her heart and her conscience were chilled, too; only her passionate longing for more than had come to her all these years, her longing to cast off her widowhood before it was too late, kept her from a plunge into despair. As she came near home she saw Jamie and his dog running ahead of her on the track. It was always strange to watch him unseen, for then it was clear how he lived in a world of his own creation that had nothing to do with everyday matters, nor with his infirmities. He talked and laughed as he ran, and it was as if the dog talked too, turning back every now and again to grin with loving eyes . . . For a second Dorian did feel a snatch at her affections. Then she saw her son with the eyes of old disappointment and dislike – a wild, dirty boy, drooling a little when he let his mouth hang open in an effort to hear and to understand . . . She shuddered and put the thought of him away from her. She had no need to think of Mallory, for between them there was not, and never had been, any love at all.

As if to prove her own indifference, Dorian kicked up her horse and went fast down the track, scattering Jamie and Brave into the undergrowth, the boy shouting with fright, the dog barking wildly. She went on without a pause, laughing. Behind her the child and his dog crouched on the ground, huddled together for comfort. But Dorian did not look round.

Mallory was crossing the yard as her mother rode in towards the stables. Dorian dismounted and chucked the bridle to Mallory.

'See him stalled. I'm tired.'

'Where'd you get, ma'am?' Mallory asked. 'Roger was all for finding you and bringing you home.'

'Roger? Why?'

'To listen what he must tell. Didn' he say he'd a long tale for us? And it was to be at a council of all us. A parliament, Edmund said – and made my brother Roger look a shade sworly! One more to this household took good sense for his thinking!' Mallory said, sticking out her chin. 'I never could like Edmund being a Cavalier.'

Dorian would not be provoked. She was less concerned with King and Parliament than with herself. She had moved of her own choice into a world narrow and perilous almost beyond bearing. She swung her shoulders as she went indoors. If she must die in a gutter, she would have her last delight of life . . .

They were having their council, or parliament, or whatever they cared to call it, seated by the big hearth in the hall. As Dorian came indoors, Cecilia called to her.

'Come listen quick! Our cousin have such a tale to tell!'

They were all attending to Roger so raptly that Dorian's curiosity would not let her turn away. She moved slowly nearer and sat down to listen.

'So I came only to see matters settled here – as I had supposed,' Roger was saying. 'Though for sure the settlement come strangely in the end. Lord – how we are tied, all of us, to the long strange past – and no way to cut the string, that I can ever see. When first I looked again on Mantlemass – I wished only to stay.'

'Shall we not all, each and every of us, stay at Mantlemass?' Edmund cried. 'Though you have a new home – '

'What home?' asked Dorian.

'Why, madam, far away,' Roger said, turning to her. 'My brother and I are settled in the New World. We sailed as soon as ever he left Mantlemass and joined me. We do well, trading and sending cargoes to many parts. Our home is in the east, on the coast there – and my brother Simon remains still, though I'm come to England. We need more settlers – I am come to get funds subscribed. I've a ship fitting out now at Gravesend.' He looked round at them, at their rapt faces, as they listened now at first hand to a tale related only distantly before. 'It's a long journey, and can be very bitter,' Roger said. 'Twice I've made it – and shall make it again. But all journeys end.' He suddenly flung out his hands to Nicholas in a generous, strangely moving gesture. 'Come back with me. There are such riches there. I have a good, stout vessel waiting, with a master of skill and courage. Come with me, Nicholas! Leave Edmund to his Mantlemass and we'll build another in another world! Set up your own family there with Pleasance – make your own line – that'll not be threatened by others claiming rights above you! Cecilia – you are steadfast and brave enough to bear that journey and find its rewards – I know it! Let us all go together, then! Nicholas – have you listened?'

'To every word.' Nicholas smiled and took Pleasance's hand, for she was looking very startled. 'Edmund's not settled long enough to master the place alone. Besides – we mun have our home here, Roger.'

'What shall come to you when Edmund's true master?'

'Why, when he gets his own family and need us leave – there's still the old foundry house standing at Plashets – though it need to be sprugged up somewhat. Didn' our great-granddam or some-such dwell there, sister?'

'No. She dwell at Strives Minnis,' Cecilia answered. 'And hung the Lily above that door.'

Dorian said nothing. She heard them tossing past and future from one to the other and knew that already she had moved apart from them. She had only to wait patiently for the word Henry Stapley would send; she need only conclude her part of a simple bargain.

11

'A great crowd of men . . .'

Roger Medley still stayed on at Mantlemass when Easter was past. Twice he rode eastward to oversee his venture and returned with glowing tales of the ship's fitting and provisioning, of her fine rigging, her sails being stitched in the lofts alongside the quay. She was a veteran of the run; her complete re-fitting was an insurance as well as a luxury.

'We shall need many new settlers,' Roger said. 'Needs must, if the colony is not to fail. So I long to make the journey less severe – we need sober citizens, not those only in flight from justice or injustice!'

'What a seafarer you are become, cousin!' Cecilia said.

'You shall tell me if any Medley before me had wandering in his blood.' He smiled at her in a way that had grown on him lately, that troubled her. 'My barque is already named – she is *The Happy Return*. If it were any way other – I might call her *The Cecilia*.'

'And I take that most kindly,' she said, lightly enough. 'So when next a gale blow out my skirts and carry me across the forest – I'll think I'm a fine ship sailing.'

'Come back with me,' he said.

'Why – how could I?'

'You know well how you could. We should be married, my dear.'

Cecilia shook her head, hating herself for it.

'Why not?' he asked.

'Better cousins do not wed. You know that as I do. Most of all, maybe, in this family. There's many imperfections.'

'All families are so . . .'

'Our grandmother writes very sternly of this. She lists such things, Roger. As stammers and high shoulders, or foolishness in some measure. Right back, so she writ down, to her grandfather's grandfather. And her own mother was crooked, more or less.'

'Many children are born this way or that,' he insisted. 'Not all. There'd be enough born straight and firm, cousins or not.'

'I cannot. Forgive me. Truly, I cannot.'

'But you do not hate me?'

'Never!'

'Then the journey frightens you –'

'That, too.'

'– And, besides, you have another in mind . . .'

Cecilia did not answer. What should she say? It needed two minds thinking alike to settle her happiness; and she knew only how her own inclined. And since John Verrall had become a fighting man, might she never see him again? Though the battleground had shifted away from them here in the south-east, the conflict broke out elsewhere, and all the time there were men fighting and dying who might be he.

'If things were otherly, Roger,' she said, looking at him honestly and squarely. 'And if you need not sail across the world – then perhaps, even though we do call cousins, I could answer you different.'

'Well – I can rest on that,' he said. He looked neither sad, nor displeased, but curiously buoyant. She knew he had thought *That man may die before I leave England* – and that he did not doubt his power to persuade her to the journey. 'Next week I must quit Mantlemass,' he said. 'I have to set about the next part of my task. There are many seeking a passage and they have all to be met and talked with. It must take some weeks. But I shall ride this way again before I sail.'

When at last he left them, even Dorian was sad to see him go. He had a steadiness, a courage, a humour that made her feel shabby spirited – almost as if she might have saved herself from disaster had he stayed.

It seemed very quiet once he had gone, taking with him in his baggage a replica of the Plashets Lily that Henty had delicately wrought for him at his request. 'I'll never wish confusion to Plashets iron,' he had said as he left. 'But I'll not pray for it, either. I wish we might all have thought samely.'

Yet there came out of his visit a union between Nicholas and Edmund that would go deep with time, if time were allowed. Now Edmund was the pupil, willing, devoted – entirely home at last, master in name, though he was still a minor in law, apprentice by good sense. They had great pleasure in one another's company.

Work went ahead steadily at Plashets. There was a good head of water in the pond and the weather lent itself to this work. An increasingly trained and disciplined army was coming into being under General Cromwell – the New Model Army, it was called, and news of it spread through the countryside; news brought to the founders working in that cause, spurring them to great and greater effort. Much material now went from Plashets to London, carried to the coast for shipment, sailing first down the Iron River six miles or so westward. With demand, so the organisation increased in rhythm. There seemed no hindrance to the flow, nor did there come any further threat to Plashets, or attempt at enclosure. And if this quiet was in itself a matter for anxiety, there was none at Mantlemass ready to admit it. They took the time and wrought it, Ben Akehurst had said, *come it ran molten for Plashets and Parliament.*

From Easter on to June all went steadily. The forest burst from a tentative green underlaid with colour, to the gushing of bracken – curled one day, plumed the next – and to the lordly dressing of such great beeches as still stood on the skyline behind Mantlemass and elsewhere. The broom was violently golden, bank on bank. That year the briar roses bloomed, Cecilia thought, as never before in her life, arching and graceful along the hedgerows that stood about the glades and tracks, tumbling without order over the edges of old quarried places. The bogs shone with the gold of asphodel, the pink of thrift and orchis. Delicate moths, small butterflies, a thousand and one forms of winged beetles and glittering flies, rose like chaff as any walked knee high through the fine grasses rich with pollen. The wild flowers were too many to be counted, from creeping woodruff to clinging woodbine, from hawksbit to heartsease and cuckoo pint; and tall angelica and fennel that Pleasance and Cecilia gathered for drying. It was a world so untouched that any could be forgiven who forgot that England was still torn in two; who heard only the birdsong, saw only a wide clear sky, and felt life gilded and enriched by the pitch and toss of daily work and family concerns. There was a better haycrop than they had seen for years, which alone raised all spirits. In the second week of June, Roger sent a messenger through from Kent with letters for all of them, a knot of fine ribbons for Mallory and a spinning top for Jamie.

'There is some delay in getting all shipshape,' he wrote to Nicholas, 'for I shall not sail with one sheet too few, or one tub of salt too small. We sail over a salt sea, yet lack of it, refined, may be our undoing.' Then at the bottom he added – 'Tell your sister my mind is steady, but I would she might change hers.'

'I cannot,' said Cecilia. Yet still, in all these months, she had no word of John.

At midsummer a man came to Plashets who had been one of a crew shipping their iron on the first stage of its journey by river. He asked first for the master. But Nicholas was not there. It was Ben Akehurst who brought him the news to Mantlemass.

'Sir, he tell me for certain sure no shipped load ever got through but the first. The master of that barge bin bought by his Lordship. The stuff got took'n carried overland – for the weather's dry and easy going, and the ground good and starky. And that's this fellow's tale, sir – that I see no need to doubt, for what purpose but truth in the telling. So – all that fine labour . . . Her's lost, Master Highwood.'

Nicholas was stunned by the news, blaming himself that he had not been more particular in his choice of freighter. But their iron had been carried by William Bowyer time out of mind. What Nicholas had not paused to recall was that *that* Bowyer had a sister married to a Bowyer of Newbridge, and Newbridge hammer thundered for the King.

'I'm a poor master, Ben,' Nicholas said. 'Time shall bring you a better.'

'Ah – there was naun to show the man scaddle, sir! Where's to find any honest man living, these days? Too, this fellow tell o' words bin spoken I needs must tell over in my turn. He have his ears wide, he say. Come they never take Plashets for the King, he say, then for sure they'll see injury to them that stands firm there. That's his tale, Mus' Highwood – and I'd think him honest.'

Nicholas frowned. 'Honest – surelye. But is it sense, Ben?'

'There was no sense in ruining the foundry in St Leonards forest, sir – yet they done that after Arundel fell. There's many see no longer, sir, than their own long noses.'

'We have our own war, then, and must needs fight how the enemy choose,' Nicholas said.

Depression settled on him. He found it hard after this to sleep easily at night. He would rise up and lean from the window, listening for sounds of danger. But the noise of one furnace or another, here or at a distance, working by night as well as day, made judgement difficult. So then he would even go downstairs and let himself out into the summer night. The air would be full of gossamer that brushed his cheek and confused his eyelashes. More than once he got his boots and went out through the night-moving forest, owls swooping, to gaze down at Plashets and pray that all was well. The silent sleeping place consoled him. Then back to reproaches from Pleasance, who feared he must tire himself out amid the rising night vapours that carried, as any knew, death-dealing contagions.

'Let be, let be, husband. Shall King and Parliament ruin all our life?'

'The danger is nearer,' he said. And added, as he had to his own furnaceman, 'We have our own war. 'Tis that goes through the forest like a plague.'

'Come now,' she begged. 'You'll frit yourself quite to death.' She put her arms round him and drew up the covers he had thrown back. 'Shall you plan to leave me a widow, like poor Dorian?'

But even his loving Pleasance could not distract him.

'Dorian . . .' he said. 'Naun much we ever learn of that last business. But does she speak of him? Of Henry Stapley, I mean. Might she see him still?'

'Dear heart, I am not her keeper,' murmured Pleasance, sleepily, tucking in close to him. 'Maybe so, maybe not . . .'

In the morning, Nicholas asked his sister the same question. What did she know of Dorian's comings and goings during these summer days? Had they been too easy – forgetting how she had smiled at Stapley as they danced together at the wedding? Forgetting earlier suspicions.

'Shall you not ask her straight out, brother?'

'You think me timmersome, I hear.'

Cecilia shook her head, smiling, but there was some slight hesitation in her manner, and he knew it. He felt again many old reserves he had fought, and defeated – so he had supposed – on the day he finally declared for Parliament and aligned himself with his own men. The regret and the frustration he had known until then – of not being Medley by name – returned to him, increased a thousandfold; for he felt now that he had no name at all. If only Roger had been content to settle at home instead of oversea – even with that difference of loyalties to stand between them, might not he and Nicholas and Edmund, the true Medley of them all, have acted in consort to grow powerful again in their own countryside?

'I shall speak to Dorian,' he promised his sister; and himself.

Only before he could spur himself to the difficulty of bringing this about, the whole of life was changed. The world fell about them.

Half-way through a moonless night, Dorian came hammering at the bedchamber door.

'Nicholas! Nicholas, wake up! Wake! I must speak with you!'

He had only just fallen asleep after long hours of brooding and self-searching. He had difficulty in deciding where he was. Then he found Pleasance shaking him by the shoulder before she sprang from bed and let Dorian in. He pulled his gown round him and fumbled for his shoes.

'There are men all about!' Dorian cried, 'There are men marching through the forest! A great crowd of men marching . . .'

'Have you been dreaming?'

'Look for yourself! Look from the window! Listen!'

'What men?' Pleasance demanded, braiding her hair as she spoke, as if she would go straight out into the dark to do battle.

'Sshh!' Nicholas breathed, awake at last. He put back the casement gently and leant out, straining his ears. Then he heard it. The sound of – how many? a score? two score? – quite a force. As far as was possible on any forest track, they were marching and orderly. There was no sound of voices, only those smaller sounds of boots on uneven ground, of leather jerkins creaking through the extreme quiet of the last hour or so before dawn. They were passing perhaps no more than a hundred paces away on the open forest. Then someone came up to them on horseback, and there was jingling added, and a voice so quiet, so near a whisper, that all the stealth of the matter was at once betrayed.

Pleasance heard it, too. 'Who?'

'We shall find out. Rouse Edmund – tell him to dress, and fast about it. Dorian – wake Giles and the rest.'

'In my nightgown?'

'Then call my sister – she'll not be so nice – or so stupid,' Nicholas said grimly. 'No light, tell her.'

They began to hustle, then, Dorian moving light-footed to wake Cecilia, Pleasance running to rouse Edmund. Gradually a stir came over the place, the house turning in its sleep, then waking, whispering; then voices coming uneasy out of the dark through which they stumbled, gradually defeating the dimness, judging all movement by the starlight filtering through uncurtained windows, broken and dimmed by drifting cloud.

'No lights – no lights!' Nicholas urged. 'Giles, are you there? Is Humfrey with you? Pleasance – did Cecilia run to the farm? Is that you, Edmund?'

Now Cecilia came back, the men from the farm were hurrying in. Mallory stood in a doorway, sleep in her eyes, her bare feet curling against the floor, cold in spite of summer.

'Is Prince Rupert come?' she mumbled. 'Is it the King? Shall we fight them?'

'Where's Jamie?' Cecilia asked, coming back in doors with Walter and Matty and half a dozen more. 'Find your brother, Mall – he'll be sore frit.'

'What's to do this time, cousin?' Edmund asked, still only half awake. 'Shall it be more enclosing?'

'We'll find that out. But let no man be too sharp,' Nicholas ordered, raising his voice as he saw them all gathering. 'Maybe his Lordship moves King's men under dark – maybe not, but we know he's gathered 'em. Now – quick and no blundering to see Plashets safe, whatever else goes. I'll not have any belver nor bannicking about, save only it's to cherish what's ourn. We go quiet – we go honest. For if naun's threatened – then we come quiet back as if we ne'er set forth.'

There was some murmuring among them, and he trusted it was of agreement. All seemed in good heart, none grumbled at losing sleep, but rather they rolled their sleeves and flexed their shoulders. 'What weapons, master?' someone said.

'Staves and fists. No iron. No steel.'

This time he thought the murmur less approving, but there was no time to be concerned or to argue.

'Open the door,' he said to Cecilia.

'We'll follow down –'

'God forbid!' cried Dorian, and half screamed.

'Dorian is right. No women.'

'We did well last time . . .'

'No women, sister. Not this time.'

So then Cecilia pulled open the heavy door and stood there holding it as the men streamed out. They moved with the stealthy quiet of accustomed poachers, light-footed, breathing easily but deep, hats, caps pulled low over their brows, in some cases almost meeting beards and so dispensing with the tell-tale pallor of uncovered faces.

'Stay close. I do order that,' Nicholas said to the women, as he left.

Edmund was at his cousin's heels. The moment they were out of doors and moving downhill, it was clear to Edmund that the night was to be different from any other he had known. This was more than the simple fact that he had never before moved through the dark with other men intent on an errand that might end violently. He had moved this way before, on the night they had thrown down the enclosure, but that night he had done no more than Cecilia and Pleasance and Mallory had done. In the end it had seemed almost a part of the wedding celebrations – it had turned into a feast, a merrymaking. Tonight's intention was keener, darker. Edmund remembered how, at home, at Ravenshall, there had hung a great dark painting of a battle, and, alongside, one much smaller, the artists's first delicate sketch for the finished picture, in which men and horses, kings and princes, fought and died bloodily. It was the battle of Bosworth Field depicted, his father had told him; where King Richard was defeated and slaughtered, where the first Tudor monarch laid the Plantagenets in the dust forever . . . It was as though Edmund moved towards such a battle, and his flesh prickled with the knowledge of what he might have to see and bear.

They came within sight of Plashets and all was silent. A faint glow from a furnace still dying at the end of its long founday was all that gave any light. None had been roused by any strange sound or threatened attack. The place slept, and so, now, the forest seemed to sleep. But just as, in a graveyard, the spirits of those gone seem strong and ready to lift the very stones that force them into the earth, so now it was most strangely certain that the night held more than stars; the dark hid more than trees and grass, the forest breathed with more than its own pattern of sounds so quiet they went almost unheard. The Mantlemass men crouched and waited on the bank above Plashets, none speaking even to his nearest neighbour. The light increased, not yet skyward, but in the eyes of the watchers, growing moment by moment more kin with the nocturnal animals going about their concerns. When a twig snapped, it was snapped by a passing fox, not by a man.

The quiet seemed likely to hold for ever. It was almost certain that whoever had passed had now moved on a different journey. Yet still the curious spell, the sensation of sharing the night with other flesh persisted among the watchers. If they relaxed at all it was only to shift position and then to freeze again. Someone stifled a yawn – it was Giles's boy, Humfrey, yawning not with sleepiness but with excitement.

'Listen . . .' Edmund said, merely breathing it.

This time it was a badger snuffling his way home, pausing to scent them, then continuing unswerving the accustomed trail to his own sett. The night was very warm, vibrant, since they had stayed so long quiet, with the churring of a ground-tit trying its feeble best to imitate the nightingale. The faintest breath of wind shifted gently through the night, sure signal that the darkest hour was almost past.

Nicholas spoke close to Edmund's ear. 'I made a boffle, could be . . .'

'No – listen . . .' Edmund said again.

The tension tightened. There was some sound, at first hard to identify because their ears were by now so strained. A rooster woke and called, too soon yet for others to reply. Then, carried perhaps on that freak of wind, there was a chinking sound, then a faint scraping.

'Spades,' Nicholas said.

And instantly that first faint sound became plain to understand, for it gathered strength. It was the sound of water, slopping then trickling, then suddenly gushing loud.

'Oh my dear God Almighty!' Ben Akehurst said, on Nicholas's other side. 'They've breached through the spillway!'

At the same instant, a light appeared in a Plashets window. A casement was flung open, and a voice – it was old Hendall's – shouted out, 'Who's there?'

Then instantly the whole place heaved into a mad hustle. It was as though the watchers above could see into the houses, as though their roofs were off, as the top may be sliced off an ant hill. They seemed to see their fellows there below, chucking on shirts, tightening belts, fumbling into boots or running barefoot to burst open their doors. Seconds only – and the men gushed forth as the water was ruinously gushing from the pond.

'Now!' Nicholas cried.

They moved on the instant, slithering, jumping, fiercely pelting down the steep bank to fling themselves to the defence of Plashets.

Down there, the men freshly roused were stumbling in the dark, shouting, trying to order themselves. But their women folk then came running with lanterns, and two old men began mounding up brushwood to light fires. Then at last, beginning to see, the men went roaring in the direction of the pond. Someone shouted 'Help come, my mates!' as the watchers reached and joined them. Another cried 'Master's here!' And though they meant Nicholas, as Edmund well knew, yet he felt his heart and his chest swell with pride and excitement. He ran with the rest, swinging the cudgel Giles had thrust into his hand as they left the house. There was nothing of politics in his mind then. He went to do battle against King's men set to destroy what amounted to Parliament property – but all that was forgotten. The enemy was Edmund's own. The battle was so ancient he shuddered to realise it. He paused briefly, only to vomit with fear of what had to come.

They were suddenly up to their ankles in swirling water. The pond, though it lay below the foundry buildings, was yet set high in its own right. The drop, so useful in control, now turned the flow of water pouring through the breach into a torrent. Men stumbled and shouted, went down and struggled up – two young boys, falling, were swept past Edmund, who grabbed at them in vain, losing his own balance and splashing down, the water flung up into his face so that he gasped and spluttered. Then he was on his feet again, struggling to move aside and so on to higher ground. The torrent, of its nature, fanned out at the edges, and they were all making for the shallow rim of the fierce flow, then scrambling towards the holding bank, catching as they went at saplings and bushes that could help them in the haul upwards.

The sky had now begun to lighten, the short summer night had subtly paled, so that a man might see his neighbour even though he might not yet distinguish any face. As they reached the pond side, men were silhouetted against that lighter sky. Edmund could see Nicholas and hear his voice vaguely above the din, could see him pointing and gesturing. He began dragging at the hunks of stone that had been shattered to let the water through. Immediately, he was joined by others, who tried to staunch the flood as they would blood from a wound. They caught up great armfuls of bracken and stuffed them in holes, endeavouring to plaster them with the wet clay that dripped from the broken bay.

Edmund looked round him for signs of strangers. Had they indeed got clean away in the dark? It had all happened so quickly it seemed hardly possible that the culprits could have escaped so easily. When Dorian shook Edmund awake she had said. 'A great crowd of men marching . . .' Then how could they be so quickly gone? *A great crowd of men* either crashed noisily away, or were so ordered that they must take time to reassemble and move off quietly. Then had the main body waited in hiding while two or three of their number set about the breach? Were they, in fact, merely moving from their mustering point to reach the old road through to London – had they stopped briefly for an attack born of the moment's opportunity? None of it seemed sensible to Edmund, but then he did not know yet a sixth of the cuts and tracks that led deviously from point to point about this ground. It could be that the force still crouched in hiding, ready at a signal to fall upon the defenders – and might they not use muskets as readily as the troopers who had descended without warning on Ravenshall and shot his own father?

In the wet and the shadow, Edmund began to feel a curious light-headedness that came from more than mere bodily fatigue. The thought of his father overwhelmed him. He had forgotten since then what now filled him with terror – how quick and un-warned a man might die. It was as if he saw this part of his life, grown out of violence sprung from nowhere, moving now towards a second violence that could destroy it utterly. He saw, blinded and deafened by the terrible plain truth of it, that from the very first blow, death is in the air – not only strong in itself against the weak body, but willed into being by the thoughts and actions of furious men. There must be one terrible moment of encounter, Edmund thought, his mind ancient with these discoveries, when one man may step aside, but another is impelled forward to his destruction . . . He tried to shake his mind free, to clear his thoughts and even his eyes, which seemed half-misted over.

Now a whole line of them had formed a chain, and stood with their backs, the big heavy backs and shoulders of iron-dealing men, against the gradually weakening flow of water. They made them-selves into a stockade, behind which others piled and hammered and drove in stones and branches to make at least a temporary barrier. Now and again, an attempted repair broke down and the water flowed suddenly over the men's leaning shoulders. They looked then like the figures of great gods supporting some ornamental fountain in a princely park or garden. But the level was now down to the breach, and the worst danger was over.

'We could'a made better a job of it ourselves!' someone shouted out. And then there was a laugh, and the mood lifted, for though it came at a bad time, the pond should fill again even in this summer season.

'Why at all?' asked Edmund. 'Why – if not better done?'

'Surprised, maybe. Old Hendall got sharper ears than any thought,' Nicholas said. 'Edmund – get down to the platt and set the women to hot broth or summat. Another hour and the men'll be fairly knuckering with cold.'

Edmund turned as he was bid. He was ready himself to *knucker*, as Nicholas called it, to whinny and neigh with the wet and the chill. He found that the women had all in hand. Fires were lit, pots steamed above them. The smell increased his faintness, so that again he felt as if he were moving involuntarily towards some point of no return.

'Take a sup now,' one woman said. 'You look to be a shade swimey, sir. And that soused-about as I never saw yet!'

'We all are that, goody.'

She ladled broth into a bowl and he took it gladly. It went down wonderfully and checked his shivering.

'Let the sun come soon to warm us!' he said.

'So it shall,' she answered, glancing at the sky. 'Shepherds' warning, looks like.'

The sky in its last richness, in that blue so full it seems almost to billow, was touched, too, with the glow of very early morning. Well out of sight still, the sun hurled itself up the high bank of the horizon.

Edmund smiled as he supped his broth, ready to laugh at his own fears now darkness was going. Then something stirred at the back of his mind and he saw the pattern repeating itself. It was not the sun that reddened the sky, for it rose in the wrong quarter – it was not the glow of comforting warmth that shot up so high, but tall wind-carried flames. He knew, then, why there was no *great crowd of men* down here at Plashets. The breaching of the pond had been no more than a cover carried out by one or two.

The rest had waited for the tumult and then set about other work.

It was Mantlemass that burned; and in the very second of knowing it, Edmund heard a low, remembered reverberation. The outline began to fill up. The pattern swelled and shook him, carrying him on his way as far as the head of the first bank before he knew, quite certainly, what lay ahead.

12

Harvest for Mantlemass

When the last of the men had disappeared, Pleasance slid her hand into Cecilia's. The hand was very cold.

'That night it were my wedding night,' she said, 'we made a festival of all that trouble. Tonight's not like to be a festival.'

'Some silly alarm, could be,' Cecilia said. She put her arm round Pleasance and drew her back indoors. 'Lord, lord!' she cried. 'How you do tremble, poor soul!'

'I do fear men greatly come they plot and struggle. It make no matter which side – once a man get a weapon to his hand, then it all come older than sides . . .'

'Get dressed,' Cecilia said, unable to find any answer to Pleasance's fears. 'What if they need help – and we sauntering here in our bedgowns!'

'Aye,' Pleasance said, nodding and rallying herself. 'Best be ready, then.'

Though she might help Pleasance, Cecilia would not have been able to comfort herself. The alarm of being waked roughly from sleep, the strange hopelessness of these small hours of the night-time, filled her with terrors she would not name. It was utterly quiet now. Cecilia pulled the door when Pleasance was inside, but at the last she paused to listen, straining her ears, imagining

Nicholas and the rest waiting somewhere, listening, listening, too . . . Then she stirred herself impatiently and went in and closed the door.

'Where's Dorian?' she asked.

Dorian had sent Mallory to dress, and followed her from the hall – Sarah reported so. Sarah was sitting on the bottom step of the stairway in a helpless, utterly uncharacteristic way, but she rose at once when Pleasance and Cecilia came back into the hall. There was a whole gaggle of other women there, clustered defensively – Dolly and Phyllis and Martha, several women from the farm like Agnes Matthews, who was Walter's wife, with her young sister, Janet. They stood close together, some looking scared, the rest merely bewildered.

Almost immediately, Dorian came into the hall. She had dressed and looked, Cecilia thought then and remembered after, as neat and tidy as if she were setting out shortly on a journey. She swept in among them, her cheeks bright, her eyes most curiously glittering.

'I went seeing to the locks about the house. If none else have the good sense, then I must do my own housekeeping.' She rushed on before any of them had time to speak – doors were seldom locked at Mantlemass, though by long habit a key hung on the wall beside each one. 'Never a one locked!' she cried. 'Yet here we bide, the forest full of villains, not a man to look to our safety – except only Jamie Medley!' She gave a high laugh and pointed at him, hanging behind Cecilia, blank with puzzlement at what was happening. 'Can't you understand, any muddle-headed one of you,' Dorian cried shrilly, 'that we're at the mercy of every brute who steps this way?'

At this the women clustering near Sarah, looking awed and respectful before Dorian's ranting, began to cry out in terror. Phyllis quickly became hysterical and had to be slapped and shaken by Sarah.

'Why do you speak so?' Cecilia said angrily. 'What gain to have them all frit to death?'

Dorian began to pace up and down, twisting her hands together, crying, 'My head aches! How shall I bear this night? How shall I bear this night?'

'As the rest of us – with moderate patience,' Cecilia answered, short and biting. 'And let us all be calm,' she cried to the women, 'and pray that no harm come to them that's run down to Plashets. In God's name, think of them! Did any one of them seem timmersome? They did not. But went off with good hearts . . . But how if any get hurt and need tending? Shall they come back to find all us weeping and shuddering?' She was harsh as they had never heard her. She raged at them, so that Phyllis now wept quietly as a scolded child will weep, and the others looked downcast and humble, biting their lips and trying to perk up their spirits. 'Let us take thought,' Cecilia insisted. 'There are things to be done, surelye. How shall we say what weapons go agin' them? There could be wounds need binding. Set water to heat, then. Dolly, Sarah – take Phyllis and find what you may in the linen closet – lest we do need bandages . . . And never look so particular, Pleasance. How else shall men mend after battle, save their women bind them together again?'

Pleasance who had moaned at the word *battle*, braced herself and took deep breaths and grew more rational. They began ordering themselves for whatever might return to them. Fires were stoked, pans of water drawn for heating, old linen torn into sensible sizes and neatly folded. At first they hardly spoke as they worked together; and all worked save Dorian. She spent the time, as change gradually crept against the windows of the sparsley lit hall, just framing the barely lighter sky, pacing from wall to wall, swinging her skirts at every turn, sometimes stopping dead to cry 'Listen!' so sharply that they all started violently. Then back she went to her pacing again. Cecilia, after an exasperated glance or two, turned her back. It was easier and quicker to get on without her. This ancient rhythm, by which women, waiting and steady, prepared to receive back the warriors, soothed and sustained them all. They began to talk quietly together, sensibly discussing what might come, allowing themselves a smile at the thought that all might yet be well, that they might be laughed at for all their pains.

Jamie had fallen asleep by the hearth; Mallory, too, sent to dress, must have crept back to her bed. She had not reappeared, and they had forgotten her while they set to work. Then, very sharply as they smoothed and folded and discussed, they heard her voice. It was barely raised, yet it brought them all to their feet. It came as the strangled, unreal scream of a sleeper struggling with nightmare . . .

Cecilia and Sarah both rushed for the stairs. But as they started up, Mallory ran along from her mother's bedchamber and hurled herself down the stairway. She came down slipping and slithering, grabbing at the rail, fighting for breath, her eyes wild with fright. She fell into Sarah's arms, clinging so hard and fast she might have been trying to force herself right into her old nurse's bosom.

'What happen? What happen? Child, thee's had a bad dream! What come to you, my lamb, my lamb!' cried Sarah, rocking and enfolding her.

Mallory's strangled cries broke off as sharply as if she had slammed a door on them. She struggled from Sarah's arms and stiffened again in terror.

'Listen! *Listen!* There it go again! There's a man walking over the roof!'

Cecilia felt her blood chill so entirely that her teeth chattered. Sweat trickled coldly between her shoulderblades.

'Dreaming, Mall . . .' she said; but the words could hardly be heard.

'Hush!' That was Pleasance, and everyone obeyed, standing rigid, ears stretched for so much as a breath.

And then it did come again; a slight sound; a subdued thump. Someone walking carefully across the leaded roof of Mantlemass.

In the silence, one of the maids whimpered and was hushed. The sound broke the instant, icy fear that had struck at all of them, and released them for some action. In the last instant before they began to whisper agitatedly together, Cecilia knew that she had heard another sound. Far away from the hall, someone had spoken – perhaps in the kitchen quarters. She would have turned to Pleasance, to see if she, too, had heard – but her eye was caught by Dorian's strange, contorted face. The vision it gave her was a vision of the truth, terrifying but utterly logical. It gave her something else – it showed her that Dorian's resolve, however it had been formed, was cracking.

'Well, Dorian,' she said, not much more than whispering it, 'best you tell us what we should do now.'

'Leave . . . Leave here! Get away! You must get away . . .'

That she said *you*, not *we* showed Cecilia that the crack in her determination was not quite large enough to let her escape by it. Cecilia must act alone, and against the odds of treachery.

She grabbed Jamie's hand and thrust Pleasance ahead of her, beckoned to Mallory to follow, nodded furiously to Sarah to shepherd the rest, and went steady and fast from the hall. By the time she had reached the far door leading into the passages above the cellars, and so to a side door on the farm side of the house, she knew they had started after her without noise or protest, without any dangerous hesitation. They brushed past Dorian as they went, not looking at her, and she backed slowly away towards the main door that would let her out into the bare dawn to take whatever way she had chosen. Cecilia did not so much as glance back at her, though she knew well they were unlikely ever to meet again; perhaps, indeed, her name would never be spoken between them when she was gone. She would have blotted herself from their thoughts . . .

At first Cecilia's impulse was to get everyone outside and then to scatter widely into the forest for shelter. But as they went through the house, it seemed to her that noise was increasing throughout the rooms they had left, and she realised they had no idea what the forest held – what men, and how many? They must surely get indoors somewhere and keep together, lest one or another got into difficulties and called for help, and the choice might be between abandoning her or risking all the rest. Her mind was clear, and she thought she could rely on those that followed, or most of them, for even frightened Phyllis seemed calm and was quiet now.

Cecilia put her hand on Pleasance's shoulder and said very softly in her ear, little more than mouthing the words, 'The Chapel Barn . . .' Then she repeated the words to Sarah and heard them sighing back among the rest.

The barn was some little way across open ground, but there was still only a vestige of light, and the distance between the two buildings had become in the last too-neglectful years covered with gorse and bramble. If there were a man still on the roof, he must see them as they moved across. But he might by now have joined his fellows who had most surely come in by the kitchen entry, and then there would be time and opportunity for escaping unseen.

Then, as they came to that door which opened into a narrow courtyard, the final exit in its far wall, Cecilia remembered something and barely forced herself to stay calm. She remembered that Dorian had gone about the house 'seeing to the locks'. A terrible picture flared into being – of the crowd of them, twelve or fifteen, or however many they were, she hardly knew – bottled up before a locked door with an enemy behind them intent on God alone could know what horrifying mischief.

It was dark in the passageway. Still thrusting a shivering Jamie ahead of her, Cecilia slipped past Pleasance and her hands ran blindly up and down the wall beside the door, seeking the key. She found its hook, but nothing hung there. In despair and terror, she shoved wildly at the door. To her amazement it opened to let them through. She knew then that Dorian had made certain all were still unlocked, that whoever might choose to enter would be free to do so. That had been her part in the business, and her reward was easy to guess.

Cecilia stood by the door, Jamie hanging on to her skirt, and saw the rest of them through and out into the morning air. Then she pulled the door behind them all and followed them as they moved slowly and cautiously across the open ground towards the barn. The enormous door stood open, but it was hanging on its hinges. It took six or seven of them to get it shut, and to thrust up the great iron bar and drop it into its slots. Of the other doors, two were already shut and barred from within. It was the fourth, a small postern door, that closed from outside. That, too, was hanging, but they could still use it, if need be, for a desperate escape, since it was more or less obscured from outside by dense elder scrub grown up against it. A vague surge of relief stirred among the women, as the bar fell across the big door – a terrible measure of how little they were ready to be thankful for. They stood under the sagging, split roof, huddled together, yet already looking hopeful.

Getting the huge door shut had made a lot of alarming noise, quite enough to betray them – only now there were so many and such loud noises coming from within the house. There was a great shouting suddenly and a wild clatter of hoofs, as the horses were turned from the stables and rounded up to be driven away. At this Agnes burst into bitter tears. 'What'll Walter do? What'll Walter say? He love and care for each and every, mane and tail and all!' But no one answered, for they were gazing through the gaping thatch, watching the sky light up.

'Mantlemass . . .' Cecilia said. She repeated it over and over. 'Mantlemass . . . Mantlemass . . .' It could have been the name of a favourite lost child. Then the ground shook to the thud of explosives, and plaster and old straw scattered down on them standing below. For a moment it seemed as if all that was left of the barn roof must fall in upon them. The dust made them helpless with coughing and sneezing, their eyes streamed. But the roof miraculously held.

Cecilia stood by the big door and pressed her face against a great crack, and saw the flames shooting. They must be running about the place with flaming torches, for even allowing for the violence of the explosions, destruction came swift as thunderbolts . . . She thought of the writing table, of her grandmother's letters, of the little iron-bound chest – that very small garnering of Mantlemass and Medley. She seemed to be weeping inwardly, the pain was so great, and she hammered with her fists against the door, unable to contain or control her despair . . . She heard Pleasance saying something, but could not take in what it was, for it sounded far away. Then Jamie's name came out of the confusion, and she shook her head to clear it and paid what attention she could.

'He ran through like a rabbit,' Pleasance was saying. 'He bolted right through the little door into the brakes and briar, sister . . .'

'Oh poor Jamie – so fearful! He ever hate such loud noise – worse'n thunder!'

'It was his dog. He did hear Brave barking, so he say – and must get to fetch him in.'

Edmund knew vaguely that a great cry had gone up from the direction of the pond. He did not wait to see men gather and change course. He knew they could not leave the breach unhealed, even with the water now so low; the bank must be strengthened. That meant not all could drag themselves, wet and weary already, towards any attempt to save Mantlemass. The confusion within Edmund's mind was increasing. When he fell after grabbing at the two boys in the water, he must have struck his head without knowing it. It ached fiercely, and that along with sheer fatigue was working a strange ruin in him. As he struggled back through the forest he did not certainly know whether he went towards Mantlemass or away from Ravenshall, whether he was himself or his own father. He moved slower with every second, his feet were the feet of a dreamer clogged in strange boglands, moving sluggish over land that moved forward with them. He struck his hand against a boulder and felt the great ring that bound him to Mantlemass shift at the blow and threaten to fly off his finger. He peered down, frowning, and it seemed to him that the ring was worn as he had so often seen its fellow, not on his own hand, but on his father's.

Well on his own way, a score or so pounding with him, Nicholas kept shouting out, 'Where's Edmund Medley? Has any seen my cousin?' and using up valuable breath as he did so. Not only was the homeward run up hill, but the incline was steepened by their weariness, even by the weight of their wet clothes. Once or twice, Nicholas bellowed Edmund's name fruitlessly into the grey morning, so sharpened and beautified by the flames ahead. He did it, perhaps, because he dared not call on Pleasance, on Cecilia, for fear they were already dead. He was not a man to curse much, but he cursed that morning. He cursed the times that allowed a man to wreck and kill for his own gain all under cover of loyalty to a cause. He cursed the Earl by name, and Henry Stapley, who was his agent. And finally he cursed Dorian, his kinswoman, his uncle's widow, for he never doubted who had helped to bring this business off so neat.

'Sir, sir!' said the smith, Hendall, striding at his side, 'Save your breath for better work.'

'What if my wife and all my children to come from her burn wi' Mantlemass?' Nicholas shouted. His face and hands were slimed with clay and with blood from tearing at great stones. He had given everything he had to work as the rest worked down at the pond, but that was gone from him now. He was utterly spent, and sick with the knowledge of what it meant to be less than a

Medley, less than a master, to lack that last fibre that measured up to iron.

As they came toiling and panting up the last track and across the river to the house, they slackened and hung back. A terrible low groan came from them as they halted. Nothing could save Mantlemass, nothing could save anything within Mantlemass. A score of men must have fired it from a score of chosen places. It was racked and battered by continuing explosions and the flames passionately consumed it. Already the windows had mostly melted and gone, the roof was falling as they looked, cascading molten lead. Here was a furnace finer and stronger than any ever built upon the forest, and it smelted out the ore of its long past so that it ran hot and hissing over the ashy ground to leave behind for the future only a tumble of cooling shapeless slag.

Nicholas fell on his knees and put his face in his hands, and seemed to sink into himself in his anguish. The man beside him shook him by the shoulder, trying to rouse him, as others rushed by them and on towards the great pile of destruction.

'There's all the farm buildings, master! There's many could be hid in safety! There's all the great forest, sir – how many run for succour there I dunnamany hundred years gone . . .' Again he shook Nicholas, holding him by the shoulders fiercely, hauling him to his feet and shouting roughly close to his face. 'Wake up! God set his face agin despair!'

'God shall forgive me,' Nicholas said.

He shoved the man off, and then found himself alone, for they had many of them wives and daughters to seek desperately. He forced himself to look at the burning house. Now the thudding and rumble of explosive seemed over. The flames had everything their way. There was no shouting, no man in sight, nothing and no one but Nicholas and the ruin of what he knew and loved. The heat dried his soaking wet clothes as he stood there. He did indeed despair. He lacked courage even to run and find how much he had lost, he dared not think of Pleasance.

Staring at Mantlemass burning, he saw then through a blurred and dusty vision a sudden breaking of the solitude into movement. Jamie went running and staggering across the front of the house, struggling to carry his dog, that was wild with fear and fought to leap from his arms. Behind Jamie Edmund was running, his hands outstretched, as if to grab the boy and help him, or else to thrust him out of danger. Then some way behind again, he saw a horseman ride quite leisurely, looking back to the house now and then, as if to make sure this was a job well done and needing no more attention. He looked as easy as some gentleman satisfying himself that all was locked and barred of the home he was leaving behind. Then, as he wheeled his horse, he looked along the burning frontage and saw where Edmund ran with Jamie.

The rider halted. He hitched the bridle into his left hand and with his free hand drew a pistol from its saddle holster.

Nicholas opened his mouth and shouted, and dragged himself out of his nightmare to stumble forward. The sound of the shot cut off his cry. He shouted again – 'Stapley! Henry Stapley!' If it was indeed Stapley, he did not hear. He pulled the second pistol of the pair and fired again, steadily, brilliantly and wantonly. He paused long enough to blow on the barrels before sliding the weapons back into the holsters. Then he rode off, now very fast.

It seemed to Edmund that Jamie had run straight from the burning house. He had his dog struggling and whining in his arms. Edmund pounded after him, intent on taking the dog from him and hustling him to safety. That was his one lucid thought, but then the confusion closed down again, it even increased. He was himself, Jamie was his brother, Harry. He was bound to care for Harry. But then, as before, he seemed to be his own father, and Jamie was both Harry and Edmund being herded to safety.

The Chapel Barn was ahead and Jamie was already set that way. Behind, all mischief was done, the perpetrators vanished, the richer for ten or twelve horses and whatever they may have looted as they went through the house. If one still remained, it was not Edmund who knew of it. He struggled on, calling and calling to Jamie, who ran like a plover with his burden, skimming and drooping along the ground. Edmund cried out, again and again, not *Jamie!* which might have checked the boy, but *Harry!* and his own name *Edmund!* which added only terror to the pursuit. Whether they ran from King or from Parliament, Edmund was far too muddled to know. He called again and again 'Harry! Harry, *wait*!' Jamie glanced back wildly over his shoulder, stumbled and fell flat.

Quite suddenly, Edmund's feet too deserted him. He tripped, hurled forward and down by a blow to the back, between the shoulder blades. Someone had struck at him with a great cold hand that seemed almost to dismember him. He lay sprawled and gasping, heaped over a whimpering Jamie. Then the blow came again, only this time it struck at his cheek.

'Go now,' he just heard his father's voice saying. 'Go *now* . . . To Mantlemass . . .'

Whether or not there remained most hideous danger, the barn door had to be opened. It had been hard to close, it was harder still to force open. The women shoved and pushed until there was a crack large enough to be squeezed through. Cecilia and Pleasance went through together, but fast as they ran another of them was faster. By the time they came to fallen Edmund and Cecilia had snatched Jamie, howling and almost bestial, into a close embrace, Mallory was already there.

She had thrown herself flat on the ground beside Edmund, flinging her arm across his shoulders, pressing her cheek against his, that was only a little bloodied, for the second shot had grazed by. There was not much blood, either, oozing from the neat hole cut by the first in his jerkin, then his shirt, then his flesh and bone and lung.

Cecilia thrust Jamie towards Sarah and reached out for Mallory, but Mallory pulled away. 'Dearest . . .' Cecilia cried, and meant it, though she had never thought of Mallory very warmly. Mallory sat back on her heels and clasped her hands together, flung back her head and cried – whether as a child robbed of its playmate, or as a woman whose love has been snatched by death, they might perhaps never know. 'Dearest, dearest Mall . . .' Cecilia cried again. The tears poured down her own cheeks, but she could not have said which of them she wept for the more. 'Oh Mall – please; please!'

'Let be,' said Mallory. 'Let be!' And again she cried out and then was silent. Then she said, so quietly they hardly heard, 'He's dead. Take him away.'

Now the others were all about them, Nicholas with Pleasance in his arms, the women and the men greeting and weeping with one another, then gradually leaving their own relief to cluster round Mallory and Cecilia as they crouched together by Edmund's body. Presently one of the men turned him gently on his back, and his mouth was open as if he still shouted a warning, but his eyes were comfortably closed; and in a way, alongside the shout, there was some sort of smile. At the sight, Mallory could not hold back a shaky laugh herself, and then turned aside to weep quietly against Cecilia's shoulder. It was a bitter end to a bitter night. Though the sun now struck so warmly over the horizon, they saw only the glow of Mantlemass and soon that would die, leaving a blackness too cold even for the sun to warm. What remained of all that life had stood for, none at that moment could have said, nor what beginnings could ever hope to blossom in such dreadful dust.

As they turned Edmund over, his hands trailing, his head lolling, something fell and rolled along the ground. It was the ring, *the lark and the laurel*, too big for him, yet worn for all it signified.

Cecilia groped for it and held it for a second very close within her shut palm, for it seemed all that was left of all of them. Then she stretched out and took Mallory's limp hand in both her own. It was a hand too childish and frail yet for so large an emblem. So Cecilia slid the ring over the girl's thumb and held it there, fast and hard – so hard that she struggled and cried out, 'It hurts! It hurts!'

'It must do,' Cecilia said. 'But not for ever.'

The sun came up strong, the sky was clear as divinity, the flames sank a little over Mantlemass.

Grandmother, grandmother! Cecilia wailed within herself, alone as she had not been since the day the secret chamber in the writing table flew open and gave up its treasure.

13

'Planta Genista'

In the warm summer weather it was possible to stay in the Chapel
Barn for shelter. A few farm buildings had been damaged, where
flying sparks had set thatches flaming, but on the whole the escape
there was remarkable enough. Half a dozen and more of the tenantry families were for occupying the barn themselves and giving
their own roofs to Nicholas and the rest. Nicholas would not have
this. His mood was sour and strange. A number of men set about
repairing the barn and getting the roof thatched, but it was Cecilia
or it was Pleasance who thanked them. Nicholas and Pleasance,
Cecilia and Mallory and Jamie lived there with a few salvaged
possessions – a stool or two, the great heavy settle from the hall,
scorched and cracked but still oak enough for defiance – some
kitchen goods, pots and ladles – very little more. Not an ash was
left of Ursula Medley's writing table and what it had contained;
and they found only the twisted lock of *the smalle chest*. The years
of their growing were taken from them utterly.

Before winter, before autumn even, they must plan themselves
a new life, a new mode of living. For the present it was not so
much lethargy that kept them where they were, existing like va-
grants, it was the dread of leaving forever the ground they had
cherished, from which they had sprung. The dank sad smell of

burning stayed in their nostrils, and when a soft wind blew the ashes of their home fell powdering upon their hair.

Not one among them ever spoke of Dorian . . .

They buried Edmund with the other Medleys and the Mallorys down in Staglye church. A stranger had come to minister to the parish, and his words were harsher than any spoken over a Medley coffin till now. Truly he spoke of resurrection, but hell seemed dearer to his heart. Heads bowed more sad than submissive, perhaps; but in Cecilia's heart, and in Mallory's, there was a great lack of meekness. The burial purged them, however, as such occasions will. Turning from the place, they did turn, Cecilia thought, to some fresh beginning. She walked away holding Mallory by the hand, drawn to her in a sympathy she would not put into words. Mallory seemed like a little widow, and Cecilia added the girl's loneliness to her own, in some measure easing both burdens . . .

'You said to Roger once that, come the time, you'd settle to live by Plashets, in the old founder's house,' she said to Nicholas that evening. 'Well, then – I'd say the time come already.' She looked anxiously at his defeated, weary expression. 'We have to speak of these things, brother.'

'So we shall,' he said.

'And then, one day, build Mantlemass new?'

He shook his head, but said nothing, leaving her with the sad certainty that he would take very long indeed to recover from this blow.

'Roger must be let know what come about,' she said, trying to rally him.

'Aye, surelye. I'll ride that way – next week, might be.'

Though in a way she had dreaded it, and knew that Pleasance had dreaded it, too, Cecilia had wanted to hear Nicholas speak of revenge. The men at Plashets and the farming people had expected it. That he accepted disaster was noble, perhaps, yet it showed the weakness he had so long tried to overcome. Those who depended on him now, those who over generations of his family and their own had depended on Mantlemass for their living, watched him uneasily. Unless he asserted his long rights over this ground, he and all of them had as well, by his default, accept the status of mere squatters, scratching what living they could, working where they might, too often moving on. Then in the future Mantlemass would be no more than 'a great house destroyed at the time of the war between King and Parliament'. Then, too, what had been so close and good-living a community, starting very small, moving by way of simple skills – the farming of coneys for fur, the breeding of fine horses – to the harshness and splendours of iron; growing from the industry and devotion of resolute and energetic men and women matched fairly to their times, would crumble and be dispersed like last year's litter. Times might change for their eventual betterment, but all they could see now was the end of everything they had known, bitterly reflected in Nicholas Highwood's defeated eyes.

Cecilia woke early one morning of high summer. She lay in the corner of the barn that she shared with Mallory, and heard Nicholas stirring. He had dressed and was pulling on his boots – a sound hard to describe and unmistakable. Cecilia sat up on her rustling straw mattress and called him softly by name.

He came across to her, treading lightly, for Pleasance still slept, as did the two young ones. Nicholas crouched down beside his sister and spoke close to her ear.

'I got lent a horse by Ben, I'll be gone two, three days – a shade more, could be. Take care till I come home – if I have a home.'

'You have a home while Pleasance lives, and while I live.' She looked at him anxiously. 'Where're you bound?'

Nicholas hesitated a second, then he said he was to ride to Roger Medley at Gravesend. 'We did say he should be aquaint wi' what happen here.'

She broke out, much alarmed – 'But it's more nor that – I see it clear!'

'Hush, now – we'll talk another time.'

'What if he sailed by now –'

'He promised to ride this way for farewells. So he would. Look after Pleasance for me.'

'Shalln't you even tell her where you're going . . . ?'

'She knows, my dear.'

He kissed her cheek and left her. She said no more, but watched him open the door and let the faint morning in, then close it and walk away. After a while she heard a horse move off from somewhere in the direction of the farm. Giles would hate Nicholas riding off alone, but they were starved of horses now. The borrowed nag would be a poor sad mount for Nicholas after Garnet. And she spared a thought for stolen Garnet riding, perhaps, to some battle his own master would abhor, and wretchedly dying in anguish there on the field . . . But mostly Cecilia thought of how Nicholas had said *She knows*. They were man and wife and must plan for themselves, but it went deep and sore with Cecilia that they had told her nothing of what they had discussed together. She knew they would never cast her off, but they would expect her to go where they went. In losing Mantlemass, though she had been no more than an unwed sister in the household, Cecilia had lost her own standing. For years she had been the strong one, buoying up her brother through his difficulties, stern with her mother when need be, with Dorian often; loving poor silly Jamie, who most needed it, tolerant of Mallory. She knew well what Nicholas could be plotting and she was deeply alarmed. It terrified her to realise that he might return to them with all plans made. They would leave England, braving the terrible journey, and start life again on that strange and distant shore. And it would be for her to marry Roger, as he so much wished.

Cecilia spent that day almost in panic, not daring to speak of the matter with Pleasance, and feeling, in any case, that Pleasance was avoiding her. She roamed through the ruins of Mantlemass, peering and picking as if she would find some hidden treasure there, a touchstone for her own escape. She went muttering lost names – Ursula Medley, Edmund, John Verrall.

It was now many months since John Verrall had travelled north, and none had had news of him, not even his old goody aunt at Staglye. With great difficulty, long ago, Cecilia had put from her the frantic distress of knowing that he had been in the house on the day her mother died, and that they had not called her to wish him even the coolest farewell. Who could say what reserves might have been thrown down if she had not been sleeping exhausted after long watching, if she could only have spoken with him then.

They would still have been parted, but she might have known herself to be waiting – while now she heard only the sad silence grown out of long absence.

Long before Nicholas rode back to the strange household in the Chapel Barn, both Cecilia and Pleasance were sick with anxiety, but still neither spoke of the cause. They had always been entirely open and affectionate with one another, so that the strain now was the more obvious, the more painful. Two days of drizzling rain added to their depression. The rain soaked the charred ruins and the air was rank with the smell of wet embers. The barn was chilly in spite of the fire burning on the stone hearth with its immense chimney breast, left from some earlier use of the place for a dwelling. Pleasance was stirring a pot over a good hot fire when Nicholas rode home, and Cecilia found it hard not to take advantage of the fact to run out and greet him first.

Instead she forced herself to cry, 'Run – run! I'll do the stirring!' and seized the spoon so forcefully that she almost shot the contents of the pot into the fire. The way Pleasance's face changed from solemnity to radiance made Cecilia deeply jealous for almost the first time since she grew up. And when they came in together the intensity of her envy shamed her.

'Well?' she said at once. 'What have you plotted for us all with cousin Roger?'

'Now, sister,' he said gently. 'Pray you – stay civil and sensible. What should we plot?'

'We all know, though it never got spoke.'

'You make me sound a tyrant,' Nicholas said. 'What's planned is best for all . . .'

'Speak it right out clear, then – so I'll know.'

Nicholas looked at Pleasance and sighed, but she was looking pale herself, and smiled back very nervously.

'Cousin Roger sets his sailing for early September. You know that much a'ready.'

'Aye – but I know naun about who sail with him.'

'Let's not get miffed!' Pleasance cried. 'Let's never quarrel!'

'I shall sail with Roger Medley,' Nicholas said, firm at least at this juncture. 'And Pleasance, who's my wife. And you, Cecilia, my only and most dear sister. And Mallory . . .'

Cecilia had returned to the pot over the fire, and the spoon clattered as she flung it down and turned angrily on her brother. 'I see. I see how it's to be. What of Jamie?'

'Not Jamie,' Nicholas said.

'Both or none.'

'Be sensible – oh I do beg you to be sensible, my dear! You know well the journey must have him frit almost to death. To death, indeed! You know, as we all do know, how early death come often to minds like his. Sarah shall care for him – Sarah and Ben shall give him his home. He shall be well provided for. Have no fear for him – you know that Sarah's heart is bigger than all ours put together.' He tried to take her hand consolingly, but she turned away, quite overcome by rage and misery. 'Understand, there's no room for all that wants to go, Cecilia. Understand that. The place shan't be took by one so smit and strange as poor Jamie. Any other could see that – and so you must, too.'

He had never before told her what she *must* do.

They argued all that evening. The talk went to and fro as they supped, as they cleared the meal between them, as they prepared eventually for bed. Last thing of all, Cecilia went out to the well up by Mantlemass kitchens, calling Mallory to go with her. The rain had stopped, it was warm and steamy with a haloed moon. Jamie tagged behind them, Brave at his heels.

'What of it, Mall?' Cecilia asked, as she let down the pail. 'What's your feeling?'

'An adventure,' Mallory said, almost wistfully, the child winning over the woman as she saw ahead of her the nameless promise of the unknown. 'And I've naun to leave behind,' she said, 'save it's Edmund's grave. I'll be glad to go from here.'

'Jamie, Mall – how shall we ever turn our backs on Jamie? How may we ever, ever leave wi'out him?'

He heard his name, as he had heard it many times that evening without understanding. He frowned and fidgeted, his mouth a little open, a run of spittle coming from the corners.

'Help me with the pail, Jamie,' Cecilia said. But first she paused to wipe his mouth on a fold of her skirt, and to run her hand over his hair to smooth it, for it was rough as a wintering pony's.

Nicholas and Pleasance were still talking when Cecilia came

back indoors. They broke off at once, and she looked at them sharply; it was certain and understandable that they had been talking about her. She would have let it go, but for one thing – as Pleasance turned to her, Cecilia saw that her eyes were full of tears.

'What now?' she asked.

Nicholas answered her. 'You'd best know. I had news in Kent of how the world goes. Sister, there was a great battle in the north, last week, it was – a place called Marston – York way. Many dead – many. Thousands, so t'were told me.'

'Do we know their names?' she asked, very steady.

'I rode by Ringmer on my way home. I needed to know what I could learn – of John Verrall, that is – and the Springetts could surely tell me. And I did speak wi' the new bailiff – him that took John's place.'

'Well?' she said. 'Well?'

'He tell me there were no hard news, only that two had seen him struck down. That he fell from his horse in the press. It do seem most certain none come forward to speak of it that saw him again.'

'I'd need to see him dead,' Cecilia said slowly. 'I'd need to see him dead as we saw Edmund.' But she knew she was talking nonsense, for it was only in old tales that women searched over the battlefield for their dead. She remembered Mallory saying *I'll be glad to go from here.* The words moved slowly through her mind. She might need to speak them herself . . .

'Cecilia . . . ?' Nicholas said.

She sighed. 'I'll be glad to go from here.'

There were many preparations to be made; many farewells. The Akehursts would care for Jamie gladly, happily. He had not been told, but so it was arranged. And if his dog should die, Cecilia insisted, then they must promise he should have another – at once, to comfort him. Nicholas took Ben Akehurst into Lewes, and found a lawyer, and drew up a deed that gave Plashets to Akehursts for ever. The lawyer wondered about the pond, since it was in fact, as the Earl had claimed, made on ground outside Mantlemass property. But, he said, the way things went of late, the King should have no say for the future, nor his Lordship, neither. So Nicholas signed the deed, and Ben put his mark, which was the best he could do.

They were to go to Gravesend and find lodgings there while they got themselves supplies, warm clothes and the like, spending what little they had left, borrowing the rest from Roger. They took one of the farm waggons, putting in a couple of horses that had escaped requisitioning on the night Mantlemass was destroyed, since they had been grazing out of sight in the bottom. Waggon and horses would be sold to earn them a little more before they left. They set out very early on a morning in the first week of August. Since that day when she had given in and agreed to go with the others, Cecilia had existed in an almost total silence. It was not a defiant or a sulking silence, but she had less need to speak than to think. She thought over every time she had seen John Verrall. She attempted the impossible task of dredging up every word he had ever spoken to her, every reply she had made. She thought of him as a boy, fishing the pool with Nicholas, and how often she had been sent to call them indoors. She remembered a fight the two had had, John's black eye, Nicholas's cut lip. She could not know whether she tried to find too little or too much in what she re-called – too little offered release, too much gave her great anguish of spirit – and in which should her best comfort lie?

The morning of departure was a greyish morning. Right up to the last minute the talk had been of telling Jamie, trying to explain; pretending, even, for his comfort, that they might return. But in the end none had had the courage, and Sarah was sure it was best so. For how should he ever understand why he was being aban-doned? 'He knows,' Mallory had said once; but he gave no sign, asked no question, though he was ordinarily inquisitive and he could hardly have missed the bustle of preparation.

They drove up over the high ground to the back of Mantlemass and then took the wide track east and a little north. It would be a longish journey, but the weather was mild, though it was sunless. Pleasance sat beside Nicholas as he drove them away over the forest, and Mallory, infected with a terrible excitement, chattered and gabbled as if her whole future depended on forgetting every-thing of her life till now. Cecilia, sitting above the cart's tail, closed her eyes and prayed only for the moment when she might open them on something she had never seen before and never loved.

'Oh look! Oh look!' Mallory cried, sudden and shrill.

Involuntarily, Cecilia looked up to where Mallory was pointing wildly skyward. Above them, so familiar, so unendingly beautiful that every Medley ever born must have paused at some time or other to gaze joyfully into the sky, swans on their early morning flight drew a great arrow pointing east to west. There must have been twenty of them, their long necks striving towards a destination, their great wings beating out the sad and plangent rhythm that would hang vibrant on the air even after they were out of sight.

'Wait!' Cecilia cried. 'Wait, Nicholas! Stop! Stop!'

He pulled up the horses, grumbling in an amiable way at a delay, but sympathetic because he, too, was moved by the flight.

Then he cried out in his turn. 'Cecilia. What are you doing? Where are you going?'

She had scrambled over the tailboards and let herself down on to the ground before any of them realised what she was doing. She ran round to the front and stretched for Nicholas's hand, crying, 'I cannot go with you! I cannot! I cannot!'

'Because swans flew over head? Is there some charm in it? Is it witchcraft?'

'Nicholas, I must stay.'

Nicholas hitched the reins and himself sprang down. He seized his sister by the shoulders and gripped and shook her in his fury.

'Be silent and do as I say! Get back to your place. We're done wi' argument and you know it. There's no time for more fighting.'

'All I ask is – go! Leave me! I saw more'n swans – though they come like some sign out of heaven – *and* pointed home, surelye! No help for it, Nick. We're bound to part. Here. Now.'

Now Mallory had joined them, hanging on to Cecilia's arm, imploring. Pleasance leant from her seat, too wrung even to weep, calling desperately, 'But we shall never meet again! Can we part for ever? We cannot!'

'We must, Pleasance. I know full sure we must. I should'a seen that from the first.'

Mallory stepped back and said to Nicholas, 'She wunna change.'

'But she's alone – alone!' Nicholas cried. 'Sister, you've none to care for you – none to keep you safe. You've no husband nor any man near to you. How shall you live?'

'If I mayn't wed where I will, then I'll endure what I must. But I'll endure it here – here.'

Now he was defeated. He turned helplessly to Pleasance, as if she could see him through this dilemma. But she could only cry again and again – 'Come with us! Come with us!'

Cecilia threw herself on Nicholas, clasping and kissing him. Then she broke away and began to run back the way they had come. The ground was uneven and tussocky, and she turned her ankle three times in the first few yards, but she rushed on. She heard someone shouting behind her, but she would not turn. Then Mallory, panting, drew level and caught her arm.

'Leave me, Mall!'

'No, wait – a moment, a moment! Take this – take it!'

She had been wearing the big ring on a thong round her neck, and she had dragged it off and was holding it out to Cecilia as she ran. Cecilia was bound to pause.

'It's yours, Mallory.'

'Keep it where Edmund was. Where we all come from,' the girl said. 'Keep it here and keep it safe. What if I lost it in the awful sea?'

Cecilia stooped and Mallory slipped the thong over her head. She thrust the ring into the neck of her cousin's dress, where it fell cold and heavy against her breast.

'Mallory . . . ?'

But the girl was gone, racing back to the cart, clambering aboard. The distance stretched and stretched between them, but Cecilia waited no longer to see them drawn out of sight and into a a future she would never share. She went fast on her way. Then she began to wave to Jamie, still standing on the little hump of ground where she had seen him while the swans flew over all of them. He stood without moving, and when she reached him, breathless, he said nothing, but only searched and searched about her face. She tried to pull him into her arms to console and reassure him; but he resisted. She did not know at all what or how much he might have understood.

'Now we'll go home,' she said to him, and again she reached for his hand.

He put it behind his back. Then, as she began to move away, he reached out and grabbed a fold of her skirt, and wound his fingers into it, and moved beside her, hanging on, hanging on all the way home. Even when Sarah almost fell to the ground with the shock of seeing the two of them together, he still held the cloth twisted into his hand, knotted between his fingers, like a tangle of yarn.

The strangeness and the quiet of her life then, fell about Cecilia like a soft warm cloak. Certain only of the ground she had chosen, not knowing how she might live with it, she moved about it in a curious dream, retracing, she thought, every footfall she had made about the forest in all the years since her earliest childhood. After a time, she knew that not all the footfalls were her own. She was set on a course her unknown grandmother had dictated. She went five or six miles north and east and saw against the flattening horizon of that upward plain, Tillow Holt, where Mallorys and Medleys had raised sheep. She moved west from Mantlemass, and found the scattered stones of Ghylls Hatch, destroyed, re-built, fallen again into ruin. Here, for all of a hundred years, great horses had been bred, but nothing stood to say so. So at Strives Minnis, where they had worked the iron over fifty years or so, the buildings remained like stumps of teeth in an ancient mouth. No more. Yet still the fishing pool, used but not made by man, lay fed by its old stream, gushing in winter, sluggish in summer, running round, running over the same boulders, still harbouring trout to tantalise and challenge young fishermen whose names were old in those parts . . . Cecilia waited for what should happen next, knowing well that Sarah watched her anxiously. She had feared that Roger Medley might ride in search of her from the coast. Or that Nicholas, having settled Pleasance and Mallory, would come back as if to fetch her, and the conflict would be to do all over again. But no one came. She had cut herself off from them more completely than she had supposed possible. If she was sobered, she was not saddened. She had chosen; and so they would do without her, as they had meant to do without Jamie, and perhaps by now they thought her just as mad . . . They were a good pair, too, she and Jamie, wandering many miles in lush autumn weather, feeding on blackberries and wild apples and the earliest nuts – then going home unrepentant to Sarah's scoldings.

After some time, as if he had been cunningly testing her truth and honesty, as if he believed he might now safely let go her skirt and she would not run away, as if he would trust her at last with far more than his crazy life, Jamie led Cecilia to the Chapel Barn again. He shoved aside a great pile of straw, and she saw what she had utterly forgotten while they were under this roof – the stone, with its lifting ring, hiding the secret place where, as she had long known, Jamie kept his treasures hidden. He had to lie flat on the ground to reach far enough into that dark hole, and so bring them one by one to view.

There was the spinning top Roger Medley had sent him, that he had never made work for him as it should, and now the whip was broken; and beside that many strange stones and bits of gnarled wood that had seemed to him when he found them to be like fruits or animals. Many pieces of slag from the ancient furnaces were there, shining and green and beautifully veined. There was a stone ink bottle, a leather falconer's glove found lying somewhere about the forest. Also a great collection of feathers, and half an antler, three-branched, that came out of the hole with difficulty, the tines catching below the lip of the opening.

Cecilia admired and praised, and Jamie looked pleased. But he also looked furtive, and she knew there must be more to show.

'What else?' she asked.

He flung himself down again and groped about, and brought out to the light a little ancient dagger, the blade broken, but the haft intact and twined ornamentally with what looked like a letter of the alphabet – R, perhaps, or P, it was impossible to tell which.

'Where did you find it?' she asked him; but he could not or would not remember. He was still looking at her expectantly, so she said again – 'What else?'

He took a long time to bring up anything fresh. This time it was a number of letters, shuffled carelessly together, tied with a scrap of twine. She knew the writing. It was Dorian's, and she thrust the letters from her.

Jamie was now head and shoulders into the hole. Gradually he wriggled himself back, and now he was holding something that made her cry out in excitement. He sprang up instantly, as if to dash away, but she grabbed at his ankle and brought him to the ground.

'Show me! Where did you find it? Give it to me!'

He hesitated still, holding his treasure behind his back.

'Please, Jamie – please – please!'

So then very slowly he brought his hand from behind his back, and gave into her hands at last after many long months – so many that she had abandoned all hope of ever seeing it – what had been lost. He held out to her, still a shade reluctantly, stitched into its skin packing, the book that Edmund had brought home from Ravenshall to Mantlemass – that he had lost at the end of his journey . . . That held, perhaps, the last, the only true secret.

When she had ripped off the covering, Cecilia stayed a long time crouched on the floor beside Jamie's treasure hole, holding the book and gazing at it, turning it over in her hands, yet lacking courage to open it. And lacking courage, too, to stay to see what his confidence might bring about, Jamie had fled, leaving her alone. He must have found the book almost as soon as Edmund had lost it, for it was dry and unharmed. It was very worn, its corners rubbed down, its spine peeling, but years and use had done that. As she held it, she felt with a great buffet to the heart, those other hands that had held it over the years, and turned the pages, and learned from them some secret which, at this moment, she lacked both skill and strength to unravel. She laid it on the ground before her, and stared at it a long while, summoning up spirit to open the covers and turn the pages.

When at last she felt strong enough, she found that the pages turned slowly, heavily, stiff with their own history – there was a thumbmark on the top right hand corner of page twenty or so – but whose – whose? The book was in Latin, which she could not read as her grandparents might have done, her great-grandparents even better. It was a book of Latin poems, then, and if the expected secret were held within the text, then she could never hope to decipher it. She turned it helplessly, this way and that, then came to a carefully folded sheet of paper, tied into the book with tape, very frail, cracked and likely to split into four if it were once unfolded. But she did unfold it, gently, delicately – only just then she was interrupted and she slid the thing away, slipping it under her skirts as she sat there on the ground.

She looked over her shoulder, defensive, annoyed at the intrusion on her privacy . . .

She stayed very still, then, and looked away. She forgot the book. A bitter desolation swept her. She put her face into her hands and wept quietly, utterly abandoned to grief. It was the cruellest deception ever practised, that she should have supposed in the first instant of seeing him, that the man coming into the Chapel Barn was John Verrall.

Then she sat rigid, and her mind tried to clear itself. For if it was not John, then who was it?

She took away her hands, slowly, cautiously, not to be gulled a second time. But by then he had reached her and was beside her on the ground. He stretched out one hand and laid it on hers, but tentatively, as if she might vanish.

'Cecilia? I thought you had died.'

'It was Mantlemass died,' she said. 'And you – so they said. In some dread battle. Northwards. But here – now . . . ? We're no ghosts! Are we? You and me? We've never died – and come haunting back?'

'Oh no – no! As God is my witness, I am here – and you are here. This is my flesh. And my bones. And my heart – my heart! And all of my spirit . . .' He took both her hands together and laid his cheek against them, then looked at her searchingly. 'And are you well? Not hurt? Still as you always were – steadfast?'

'If that's what you think I always bin – then yes.' Now it was she who looked so closely at him, seeing scars in his face, not set there by any weapon but by hard experience. 'And you? Speak of you and I'll tell all the rest later. Tell me again you come safe home.'

'I am so,' he said soberly, 'and much blessed in being so. Truly it was a dread despairing battle that day. Not for us – God gave us the victory. But for thousands slain of the King's side. At Marston, it was – we fought across the moor there. Thousands, thousands littered the ground – they lay waiting to be shovelled under the turf that was all bloodied – our blood and theirs, but a thousand times more theirs . . . I doubt so many of one side died in a day.' He paused and covered his eyes for a second, and shook his head as if sounds rang in his ears that could not be endured. 'Towards evening, when victory was sure, General Fairfax rode about the field, his face all bloodied, trying to stop more slaughter – crying out to our soldiers, beating up their swords – crying Spare your countrymen! Spare your countrymen! But they were past reason . . . I pray it never come to you to see men drunk with blood and death . . .'

'Over,' she said. 'It's over. You come home.'

'I lay a long while sick and sore.' He held up his right hand. 'Last time it was a gash – this time they carried off two of my fingers . . . Aye, true – I'm home. I'll never hold sword nor fire a musket from this day on.'

'I see it all in your poor face,' Cecilia said. 'That battle.'

So she should, he told her, when he was grown an old man.

She thought how nearly she had gone with Nicholas, how nearly she had lost what most she longed for.

'Oh John,' she said, 'dear John Verrall – I turned back for Jamie's sake – but God knew all along what I'd find beside . . .' She heard what she had said but forced herself not to look away since he had called her steadfast. 'I told you right out I love you,' she said. 'Which no maid should.'

Later, when the whole tale of the time between them was unravelled and re-spun, he said they should look at the book, and look at it together.

John opened it at the first page, that has the title always, and there was written the name of the book's first owner. It was *Richard Plantagenet.* Then below it, in another hand, *My father's book.* And again, below both, in the handwriting now so familiar to Cecilia, her grandmother Ursula's hand, was added: *This is the secret that come from my great-great-grandfather, son unacknowledged to third King Richard of England. His blood being carried through me to such Medleys as come after* . . . On the last narrow space of all was a thin, spidery drawing, leaves, flower, seed of the common broom that blew about the forest. *Planta genista*, Ursula had printed carefully underneath . . .

The ashes of Mantlemass seemed to rise on the wind and rain down on Cecilia.

'What shall I do?' she asked; for it was as though for a wild second the crown of England hung in the air before her.

'What *shall* you do?' he said gently. 'Save be my wife and let us be content together and forget all else. God give us life and power to live it. But who come king and who come commoner – heaven alone knoweth.'

'Shall I forget it, then?'

'I did hear something of this once,' John said. 'Old tales cling around these parts. It came of some talk, I recall, of Medley faults – such as backs and shoulders, I mean, and wits. And someone said, it all come down to them from some old king, they said, that was somewhat the same . . . It would have been that last Plantagenet, Cecilia – that Richard. But you well know that Medleys got mixed with far others than kings. Halacres, see you, who were humble weavers for the most. And Bostels – far back there was something to that. Others, too, maybe – for birth and marrying shift us back and fore till we're too dizzy to be sure where we started.'

She nodded, unable to speak just then, or look at him, she felt so lost in time.

'Look, my dear love,' he insisted, 'we're but ourselves – bodies out of the earth that bore us and the air that gave us breath, souls by gift of God. Ghosts unborn . . . What else, then? What more?'

'Nothing more,' she said, barely heard.

Yet still she looked at the book in her hands, at the strange great name out of the long past, and the paper unfolded and telling her where a man had died, and when . . . *Anno Domino 1550. Rychard Plantagenet was buried the twenty-second day of December Anno ut Supra* . . . All that she had ever learnt of Mantlemass, spoken, written, remembered, she saw now contained within this small and ancient book as in a coffin. She had spoken of a harvest once – a harvest for Mantlemass – and this was it, so small and insignificant that it had been hidden with ease even by her idiot boy.

'Shall it burn like all the rest?' she asked.

'If not,' he said, but kind and teasing only, 'shall you plan to give me – me! – the grandchildren of kings?'

Still, still she held the book and turned it and warmed it within her palms, and felt the hand of her grandmother who had held it before her, and of many more. She laid the book for a second against her breast. As she did so, she felt the great ring hanging there, pressing against her as if in reminder.

'Don't look so pitiful, love!' John cried. 'The secret is yours. I cannot take it from you. Only you may decide what best to do with it.'

'I have decided,' she said.

She would destroy the book, she would destroy it to please him. It should be the first hard proof of her love for him. The ring she would keep for her first child, son or daughter, that she had promised her grandmother's ghost should be called *Medley*.

She pulled him into shelter as she had pulled Jamie. She hugged him against her, hoping to warm him a little. She rubbed his cheeks and pinched his chin; and slapped him, though gently, for she feared roughness might finish him. A terrible anxiety filled her. She began to wonder what she should do for the best if Jamie forgot his errand and went off about his own concerns without calling help. She felt, as she held the sick boy, that she stuffed his life back into him, with great difficulty stopping up the vents by which it might drain away. She had never watched any man or any woman die, but she knew by instinct what the blue transparency beneath his eyes must mean, and the harsh texture of his dry cracked lips. She put her face against his and blew softly, as she had once seen a cow blow life into her calf . . .

Then she heard someone running up the track and knew by the weight of the tread that it was a man who came. Nicholas called her name, curious, a little anxious, cautious because it was Jamie who had told a tale to fetch him from his concerns. Cecilia called back, then heard others coming, too, and knew that her worst fears were over.

Nicholas had brought Humfrey Bostel with him; and the enormously strong Ben Akehurst, who could have carried off an ox in his arms – and done so, in fact, one Lammas fair.

'Who is he?' Nicholas asked, crouching beside Cecilia. 'Did you ever see him before?'

'Never!'

'Do you know him, Humfrey? Ben?'

'Never seen till now, not by me,' said Humfrey; and Ben Akehurst echoed him.

'Well, never mind his name,' cried Cecilia, 'he's our charge, whatever he's called. And he's powerful sick, brother.'

'He moved a little . . . I thought he moved. Look – look now!'

The boy shifted his head very slightly from side to side and muttered something.

'What's that he say, master?' asked Humfrey.

'Too faint to hear.'

Cecilia had heard – or so it seemed. One word, only.

'Mantlemass,' he had said, sighing it out. He opened his eyes slowly, as if great weights lay on the lids. He said again

'Mantlemass . . .' This time so clear that every one of them heard it. Then his eyes closed once more and he was silent.

By supper time three nights later, the sick boy had become a bone of contention to the older members of the household.

'Where's he from, I say? And where's he going? And how soon shall he be well enough to leave? And why must it be we who succour him?'

'Who else?' Cecilia demanded. She looked without love at her aunt Medley – Dorian, they all called her, as her husband Thomas had done, shortening the mouthful *Dorothy Ann*.

'Merely goods enough to keep ourselves – and now this stranger!'

'Should I have left him?'

'You never should have found him!' Dorian Medley cried absurdly. She could not abide anything that threatened her own comfort, which was thin enough these days. It was certain she had never forgiven her husband for dying so inconsiderately soon after their marriage. She had remained ever since in a state of indulgent self-pity that had turned her from a silly pretty woman into a sharp-mannered slattern drifting through life in a dirty-hemmed gown trimmed with torn lace. She despised and bullied her sister-in-law, Susan, quarrelled with Cecilia whenever she could, and tolerated only Nicholas – chiefly because he was the sole available masculine company. A great misfortune that she had not married again – and she thought so, too, but suitors did not come two a penny in these parts. For her own children Dorian had little use. Her daughter, Mallory, at twelve was too clever to be endured. As for soft-headed Jamie, his mother was alternately kind and cruel to him – kind when she needed him as a reassurance of the Mantlemass inheritance, cruel when he reminded her all too clearly that her only son was an idiot – and not from *her* family could the fault have come.

'Jamie found him,' Nicholas put in.

'Well, then, you see . . .' Dorian said, shrugging.

'And the only word he spoke was *Mantlemass*.'

'Why, for sure, he had been told it was the nearest good household to go begging.'

'He's no beggar, I think.'

'Then how shall we know he's not a spy? A spy for Parliament! And'll send his kind to take Plashets for arms, and destroy us all!'

'At least,' said Susan, 'he's a man of sorts. Rejoice, Dorian! You ever do moan that we're a pack of women here.'

'Aye, my good aunt, you should rejoice indeed,' Nicholas teased her. 'For at one blow the grown male population of this house is no less than doubled!'

'How coarse you speak! And to a lady! And you know well I shall never endure to be called aunt by a great grown lout like you!'

Nicholas laughed and glanced at his sister. It was always the way that Dorian, when she seemed so intolerable as only to be borne for the sake of family and sweet charity, would snap out some nonsense that made them smile.

'When we know more of him,' Nicholas said, 'when he is some way recovered – then we shall decide what's best to do. These are sharp hard times we live in. He's parted somehow from his own people. Maybe they go weeping for him.'

Cecilia left the rest still arguing over the end of the meal, and went to the kitchen. Ben Akehurst's wife, Sarah, was in charge there, with Dolly and Sue, and Lizzie who scrubbed the floors and swilled the dishes.

'I made a good broth,' Sarah said, 'for there's always bones with marrow in 'em, thank the Lord. And I put a handful of barley to the rest.' Like most women she found pleasure and satisfaction in feeding up a sick man. 'How is he this day, think you?'

'Better. And shall be best.' Cecilia hesitated a moment. She put a finger into the broth and tasted it, and nodded. Then she said, 'Sarah – you did see him, dirty and clean. Would you say he had a bly of my brother – do they two look alike?'

'Come you mention it, I might say so,' Sarah answered, weighing a ladle thoughtfully and turning over carefully this new idea – as she might turn a cake to see if it was baked. 'Aye, maybe. But you never saw him othertime?'

'Never.'

Sarah had known Cecilia since her childhood. She knew, now, that the girl had something more to say, and so she waited but did not question her.

33

'It sometimes come to me, Sarah,' Cecilia said at last, 'that we've kin here and there about the world by now. And how if he were one – and come home to Mantlemass?'

'He's never one of Master Thomas Medley's breed, mistress. His grandsons could only be babes as yet.'

'Nay, but long ago – well, I did hear tell of this,' said Cecilia, mumbling a bit as she sliced bread to crumble into the broth, 'well, I did hear it someways somewhen – nay, I did read it in a letter, truly, Sarah – a letter writ long ago by my grandmother . . .'

'I recall her, just,' said Sarah.

'There was a quarrel between brothers – three brothers – and the eldest went away.'

'When was that?'

'Oh, long, *long* ago,' insisted Cecilia, speaking hurriedly, still mumbling a little, for she had meant never to speak of such discoveries. 'My – my great-great-grandfather, it would have been – his eldest brother . . . But no matter about it . . . Shall we take up some of the good French wine?'

'Best so,' said Sarah; and frowned a little as she tried to parcel out the distance in time between a girl and her great-great-grandfather.

'The broth smells so good I've a mind to start my supper over,' Cecilia said. 'Sarah – I need you should teach me all your skills. I know some – not near enough. If I had need – I'd choose to know about brewing and baking.'

'How should you ever have need, my dear creature?' cried Sarah, smiling.

'My grandmother could command her house, Sarah – I could not. What if one day I should get left wi'out servants?'

'No, no – you never shall. Not while I live.'

'But we must all die, Sarah. And we do live in strange, angry times . . . Anyway, I can tell you, other ladies of this house have been greatly skilled . . .'

'Oh aye – your greatest-greatest-*greatest* grandmother, no doubt! But you've skills they never much knew, if I'm told right. How you do read b'the hour! And write, mistress! Could such dames do so much?'

'For sure . . . Well, they'd fewer books, it's true. But, dear